The Gospel According to Peter

By Walter Richard Cassels

Published by Pantianos Classics

ISBN-13: 978-1975973940

First published in 1894

Contents

I	5
II	9
III	14
IV	20
V	29
VI	31
VII	37
VIII	41
IX	93
X	96
XI	111
XII	114
Appendix - Ευαγγελιον Κατα Πετρον	*117*
Notes	*121*

Ἐπειδήπερ πολλοὶ ἐπεχείρησαν ἀνατάξασθαι διήγησιν περὶ τῶν πεπληροφορημένων ἐν ἡμῖν πραγμάτων .....

Forasmuch as many took in hand to draw up a narrative concerning the matters which have been fully believed among us....

Luke i. 1

I

Egypt, in our days, ceasing to be any more the land of bondage, has, in more senses than one, become a veritable Land of Promise. It is a rich mine of historical and literary wealth, alas! most inadequately worked, and in that fine climate, with its clear dry air, the footprints of Time, leaving scarcely a trace, the treasures of an ancient civilisation, even of the most delicate texture, have been preserved to us with wonderful perfection. The habits of the peoples that have occupied the land have happily combined with the natural advantages of the climate, in transmitting to the modern world an inheritance of which we are now beginning to take possession. The dead have long been giving up their secrets, but it is only in recent times that we have been able to realise the fact that the tombs of Egypt may contain many a precious work, now known to us but in name, and many a writing which may change the current of controversy, and strangely modify many a cherished opinion. Without referring here to earlier discoveries in support of these remarks, we may at once pass to the more recent, with which we have particularly to do.

In the course of explorations carried on during the winter of 1886-87 by the order of M. Grébaut, then Director of the Museums of Egypt, two Greek manuscripts were discovered in the necropolis of Akhmîm, the ancient Panopolis, in Upper Egypt. The first of these was a papyrus, which was really found by some Fellahs who quarrelled regarding the partition of their precious booty and thus allowed the secret to leak out. It came to the knowledge of the Moudir, or Governor of the Province, who promptly settled the dispute by confiscating the papyrus, which he forwarded to the Museum of Gizeh at Boulaq. This MS.

is a collection of problems in arithmetic and geometry, carefully written out, probably by a student, and buried with him as his highest and most valued achievement.

The second manuscript was of much higher interest. It was discovered in the tomb of a "monk." It consists of thirty-three pages in parchment, measuring 6 inches in height by 4-½ inches in breadth, without numbering, bound together in pasteboard covered with leather, which has become black with time. There is no date, nor any other indication of the approximate age of the MS. than that which is furnished by the characteristics of the writing and the part of the cemetery in which it was discovered. These lead to the almost certain conclusion, according to M. Bouriant, who first transcribed the text, that the MS. cannot be anterior to the eighth century or posterior to the twelfth. The ancient cemetery of Akhmîm stretches along to the north and west of the hill on which have been discovered tombs of the eighteenth to the twentieth dynasties, and it has served as a burial-place for the Christian inhabitants of the neighbourhood from the fifth to the fifteenth centuries, the more ancient part lying at the foot of the hill and extending gradually upward for about 700 metres. The tomb in which the MS. was found is in a position which approximately tallies, as regards age, with the date indicated by the MS. itself.1 Of course, these indications refer solely to the date of the MS. itself, and not to the age of the actual works transcribed in its pages.

The thirty-three sheets of parchment, forming sixty-six pages, commence with an otherwise blank page, bearing a rough drawing of a Coptic cross, upon the arms of which rise smaller crosses of the same description, and the letters [symbol] and [symbol] stand the one on the left, the other on the right of the lower stem of the large cross. Over the page commences a fragment of the "Gospel of Peter," which continues to the end of page 10, where it abruptly terminates in the middle of a sentence. Pages 11 and 12 have been left blank. Pages 13 to 19 contain a fragment of the "Apocalypse of Peter," beginning and ending abruptly, and these have, either by accident or design, been bound in the volume upside down and in reverse order, so that, as they actually stand, the text commences at page 19 and ends at page 13. Page 20 is again blank, and the rest of the volume is made up of two fragments of the 'Book of Enoch,' the first extending from the 21st to the 50th page, and the second, written by a different hand, from the 51st to the 66th page. Finally, on the inside of the binding, and attached to it, is a sheet of parchment on which is written in uncials a fragment of the Greek "Acts of St. Julian," though which St. Julian amongst those in the Calendar does not appear.

The French Archeological Mission published in 1892² the mathematical papyrus, edited by M. Baillet, but the much more interesting and important volume of fragments did not appear until 1893,³ when they were edited by M. Bouriant. These precious works remained, therefore, practically hidden from the world for five or six years after their discovery, in consequence of what is vaguely, but truly, described as "vexatious delays," whilst the comparatively uninteresting arithmetical work preceded them by more than a year. The fragments of the "Gospel" and "Apocalypse" of Peter, long known by references or quotations by the Fathers, make us acquainted, for the first time, with the writings themselves, and the fragments of the "Book of Enoch" give us the Greek text of part of an early work quoted by the writer of the Epistle of Jude, hitherto only extant in an Ethiopian version.

Of almost greater interest than the actual discovery of these and other precious MSS. from time to time, in a similar way, is the possibility and probability opened out to us that we may yet recover from the dead still more precious works than these. The cemetery of Akhmîm stands near the ancient and very important city of Panopolis, and from a very early period it was the centre of a considerable Christian population. The custom of burying with the dead books which were a valued possession during life was probably a survival of the same primitive custom in accordance with which also a warrior's horse and dog and his weapons were interred with him to serve him again in the world of spirits. That books, at a time when their multiplication was so slow, should have been interred with their dead possessor is not only curious but very fortunate for us, and we may yet thank the cemetery of Akhmîm for preserving safely for us manuscripts which in no other way could have escaped the effects of time and the ravages of barbarism.

The fragments with which we are dealing present some peculiarities which deserve a moment's notice. The Gospel according to Peter commences in the middle of a sentence, but being at the top of a page it is probably only part of a manuscript of which the earlier portion was either lost or belonged to some one else. The fragment, however, ends abruptly in the middle of a phrase and, being followed by blank pages, the reasonable presumption is that the scribe intended to complete the transcription, but for some reason did not do so. It is curious that in a similar way the "Apocalypse of Peter" is only a fragment, beginning and ending abruptly, with a page left blank for continuation. Did the scribe hastily copy stray leaves of each work, which had fortuitously come in his way, leaving room for more should he be able to secure the rest? or did he break off his copy of the one to take up the other, and with equal restlessness leave it also unfinished? We shall never know exactly, but considering the value of books at that epoch, the probability seems to be that he hastily copied such portions of writings as had come into his possession, time or accident preventing the completion of his task.

The fragment of the "Gospel" of course does not bear any name or superscription—nor, indeed, does the "Apocalypse"—but the title is clearly deduced from the work itself, the writer saying directly "but I, Simon Peter," and thus proving that the narrative takes the form of a composition by that Apostle. It may be remarked, merely in passing, that it is a curious—if not in any way a significant—fact that the two Christian fragments in this little volume should both profess to have been written by the Apostle Peter. Are the peculiarities of the fragments which we have described due to the passage of some one having in his possession two works selected as being believed to emanate from the chief of the Apostles, from which there was only time to make these extracts? There is some reason for thinking that the parchment may have previously been used for some other writing, obliterated to make way for these fragments. The little volume has not altogether escaped injury in its long rest by the side of the dead, and parts of the text have had to be supplied by conjecture; but, on the whole, the writing is fairly legible and, by the invaluable aid of photography, it has been copied and published with complete fidelity. Before this was done, that the first transcription by M. Bouriant should have contained errors and omissions which led scholars into mistaken conclusions is very intelligible, but the text may now be considered fairly settled, and the following is a rather close and unpolished translation of the "Gospel according to Peter."

II

The Gospel According To Peter 4

(1) ... but of the Jews no man washed his hands, neither Herod nor any one of his judges; and as they were not minded to wash, Pilate rose. (2) And then Herod the King commandeth the Lord to be taken, saying unto them: "Whatsoever I commanded that

ye should do, that do unto him." (3) But there was there Joseph, the friend of Pilate and of the Lord, and knowing that they are about to crucify him, he came to Pilate and asked the body of the Lord for burial. (4) And Pilate sent to Herod and asked for his body. (5) And Herod said: "Brother Pilate, even if no one had begged for him, we should have buried him; because the Sabbath is at hand; for it is written in the Law: 'The sun must not go down upon one put to death.'"

(6) And he delivered him to the people before the first day of the Unleavened bread of their feast. And taking the Lord they pushed him hurrying along, and said: "Let us drag along the Son of God as we have power over him." (7) And they clad him with purple and set him on a seat of judgment, saying: "Judge justly, King of Israel." (8) And one of them brought a crown of thorns and set it upon the head of the Lord. (9) And others standing by spat upon his eyes, and others smote him on the cheeks; others pierced him with a reed, and some scourged him, saying: "With this honour honour we the Son of God."

(10) And they brought two malefactors and crucified between them the Lord; but he kept silence as feeling no pain. (11) And as they set up the cross they wrote thereon: "This is the King of Israel." (12) And they laid the clothes before him and distributed them and cast lots for them. (13) But one of these malefactors reproved them, saying: "We have suffered this for the evil which we wrought, but this man who has become the Saviour of men, what wrong hath he done you?" (14) And they were angry with him, and they commanded that his legs should not be broken, in order that he might die in torment.

(15) Now it was mid-day, and a darkness covered all Judaea, and they were troubled and anxious lest the sun should have set whilst he still lived, for it is written for them: "The sun must not go down upon one put to death." (16) And one of them said:

"Give him to drink gall with vinegar;" and having mixed, they gave him to drink. (17) And they fulfilled all things and completed their sins upon their own head. (18) Now many went about with lights, thinking that it was night, and some fell. (19) And the Lord cried aloud, saying; "Power, my Power, thou hast forsaken me!" and having spoken, he was taken up. (20) And the same hour the veil of the temple of Jerusalem was torn in twain.

(21) And then they took out the nails from the hands of the Lord, and laid him upon the earth; and the whole earth quaked, and great fear came [upon them]. (22) Then did the sun shine out, and it was found to be the ninth hour. (23) Now the Jews were glad and gave his body to Joseph, that he might bury it, for he had beheld the good works that he did. (24) And he took the Lord and washed him, and wrapped him in linen, and brought him into his own grave, called "Joseph's Garden."

(25) Then the Jews and the elders and the priests, seeing the evil they had done to themselves, began to beat their breasts and to say: "Woe for our sins: judgment draweth nigh and the end of Jerusalem." (26) And I, with my companions, was mourning, and being pierced in spirit we hid ourselves; for we were sought for by them as malefactors, and as desiring to burn the temple. (27) Over all these things, however, we were fasting, and sat mourning and weeping night and day until the Sabbath.

(28) But the scribes and Pharisees and elders assembled themselves together, hearing that all the people murmured and beat their breasts, saying: "If at his death these great signs have happened, behold how just a one he is." (29) The elders were afraid and came to Pilate beseeching him and saying: (30) "Give us soldiers that we may watch his grave for three days, lest his disciples come and steal him, and the people believe that he rose from the dead and do us evil." (31) Pilate, therefore, gave them

Petronius the centurion with soldiers to watch the tomb, and with them came the elders and scribes to the grave. (32) And they rolled a great stone against the centurion and the soldiers and set it, all who were there together, at the door of the grave. (33) And they put seven seals; and setting up a tent there they kept guard. (34) And in the morning, at the dawn of the Sabbath, came a multitude from Jerusalem and the neighbourhood in order that they might see the sealed-up grave.

(35) Now, in the night before the dawn of the Lord's day, whilst the soldiers were keeping guard over the place, two and two in a watch, there was a great voice in the heaven. (36) And they saw the heavens opened and two men come down from thence with great light and approach the tomb. (37) And the stone which had been laid at the door rolled of itself away by the side, and the tomb was opened and both the young men entered.

(38) Then those soldiers, seeing this, awakened the centurion and the elders, for they also were keeping watch. (39) And whilst they were narrating to them what they had seen, they beheld again three men coming out of the tomb and the two were supporting the one, and a cross following them. (40) And the heads of the two indeed reached up to the heaven, but that of him that was led by (41) their hands rose above the heavens. And they heard a voice from the heavens, saying: "Hast thou preached to them that are sleeping?" (42) And an answer was heard from the cross: "Yea." (43) These, therefore, took counsel together whether they should go and declare these things to Pilate. (44) And whilst they were still considering, the heavens again appeared opened, and a certain man descending and going into the grave.

(45) Seeing these things, the centurion and his men hastened to Pilate by night, leaving the tomb they were watching, and narrated all things they had seen, fearing greatly and saying: (46)

"Truly he was a Son of God." Pilate answered and said, "I am pure of the blood of the Son of God, but thus it seemed good unto you." (47) Then they all came to him beseeching and entreating him that he should command the centurion and the soldiers to say nothing of what they had seen. (48) "For it is better," they said, "to lay upon us the greatest sins before God, and not to fall into the hands of the people of the Jews and be stoned." (49) Pilate, therefore, commanded the centurion and the soldiers to say nothing.

(50) In the morning of the Lord's day, Mary Magdalene, a disciple of the Lord (through fear of the Jews, for they burnt with anger, she had not done at the grave of the Lord that which women are accustomed to do for those that die and are loved by them), (51) took her women friends with her and came to the grave where he was laid. (52) And they feared lest the Jews should see them, and said: "If we could not on that day in which he was crucified weep and lament, let us do these things even now at his grave. (53) But who will roll us away the stone that is laid at the door of the grave, in order that we may enter and set ourselves by him and do the things that are due? (54) For great was the stone, and we fear lest some one should see us. And if we should not be able to do it, let us at least lay down before the door that which we bring in his memory, and let us weep and lament till we come to our house." (55) And they went and found the tomb opened and, coming near, they stooped down and see there a certain young man sitting in the midst of the tomb, beautiful and clad in a shining garment, who said to them: (56) "Why are ye come? Whom seek ye? Him who was crucified? He is risen and gone away. But if ye do not believe, stoop down and see the place where he lay, that he is not there; for he is risen and gone away thither whence he was sent." (57) Then the women, frightened, fled.

(58) And it was the last day of the Unleavened bread, and many went forth, returning to their homes, the feast being ended. (59) But we, the twelve disciples of the Lord, wept and mourned, and each went to his home sorrowing for that which had happened. (60) But I, Simon Peter, and Andrew, my brother, took our nets and went to the sea, and there was with us Levi, the son of Alphaeus, whom the Lord....

III

No one can have studied this fragment of the Gospel according to Peter, with its analogy to, and still more striking divergence from, the canonical Gospels, without perceiving that we have here a most interesting work, well worth serious examination. The first question which naturally arises is connected with the date to be assigned to the fragment: Is this a part of the work used by many of the Fathers and well known amongst them as the Gospel according to Peter? We must first endeavour to form a correct judgment on this point.

Eusebius has preserved to us the earliest detailed notice of the Gospel according to Peter extant, in a quotation from Serapion, who became Bishop of Antioch about a.d. 190. Eusebius says:

There is likewise another work written by him upon the so-called Gospel according to Peter, which he composed to refute the untruths contained in it, on account of certain in the community of Rhossus who were led away by this writing to heretical doctrines. It may be well to set forth some passages of this in which he expresses his opinion of the book:

"For we, brethren, receive both Peter and the other Apostles even as Christ. But the false writings passing under their names we from experience reject, knowing that such things we have not received. When I was with you, I was under the impression that all held to the right faith and, without going through the Gospel put forward by them in the name of Peter, I said: 'If this is the only cause of difference amongst you, let it be read.' But now, having ascertained from information given to me that their minds were in some mist of heresy, I will hasten to come to you again; so, brethren, expect me shortly. We, therefore, brethren, knowing of what heresy was Marcianus, recognise how much he was in contradiction with himself,5 not comprehending that which he was saying, as you may perceive from what has been written unto you. For we borrowed this gospel from others who used it: that is to say, from the followers of those who introduced it before him, whom we call Docetae—for most of its thoughts are of this sect—having procured it from them, I was able to go through it, and to find, indeed, that most was according to the right teaching of the Saviour, but certain things were superadded, which we subjoin for you."6

There is little or no doubt that the writing before us is a fragment of this "Gospel according to Peter" of which Serapion writes.7 It must always be remembered, as we examine the evidence for the work, that we have here only a short fragment, and that it would not be reasonable to expect to find in it materials for a perfect identification of the work with references to it in writings of the Fathers. Within the few pages which we possess, however, there is sufficient justification for concluding that they formed part of the Gospel current in Rhossus. Only one "Gospel according to Peter" is mentioned by early writers. This fragment distinctly pretends to be a narrative of Simon Peter; and its matter is generally such as must have satisfied Serapion's ideas of orthodox doctrine, if suspicion of Docetic tendencies had not made him believe that it contained a superadded leaven of heresy. This may not appear very clearly in the fragment, but we know from other sources, as we shall presently see, that they existed in the Gospel, and even here the representation that Jesus suffered no pain; that he is always called "the Lord," or the "Son of God;" that his one cry on the cross was susceptible of peculiar explanation, and that he was immediately "taken up," whilst his body subsequently presents aspects not common to the canonical Gospels, may have seemed to the careful bishop sufficiently Docetic to warrant at least his not very severe condemnation.

It is unnecessary to discuss minutely the details of Serapion's letter, which, if vague in parts and open to considerable doubt in some important respects, is at least sufficiently clear for our purpose in its general meaning. Nothing is known of the Marcianus to whom it refers. The bishop had evidently previously written of him, but the context has not been preserved. The Armenian version, made from a Syriac text, reads "Marcion" for "Marcianus," but it would be premature on this authority to associate the episode with that arch-heretic of the second century. It is clear from the bishop's words that on his previous visit to Rhossus, at the desire of part of the community, he sanctioned the public reading of the Gospel of Peter but, after personal acquaintance with its contents, he withdrew that permission. Zahn[8] maintains that the private reading by members of the Christian community, and not public reading at the services of the Church, is dealt with in this letter, but in this he stands alone. The Index expurgatorius had not been commenced in the second century, and it is impossible to think that the sanction of a bishop was either sought or required for the private reading of individuals. We have here only an instance of the diversity of custom, as regards the public reading of early writings, to which reference is made in the writings of the Fathers and in the Muratorian and other Canons. In this way the Epistle of the Roman Clement, as Eusebius[9] mentions, was publicly read in the churches; as were the Epistle of Soter to the Corinthians, the "Pastor" of Hermas,[10] the "Apocalypse of Peter,"[11] and various Gospels which did not permanently secure a place in the Canon.

Eusebius, for instance, states that the Ebionites made use only of the "Gospel according to the Hebrews."12

Eusebius13 mentions a certain number of works attributed to the Apostle Peter: the first Epistle, generally acknowledged as genuine, "but that which is called the second," he says, "we have not understood to be incorporated with the testament" (ἐνδιάθηκον). The other works are, the "Acts of Peter," the "Gospel according to Peter," the "Preaching of Peter," and the "Apocalypse of Peter," the last being doubtless the work of which a fragment has now been discovered in the little volume which contains the fragment of the Gospel which we are considering. Of these Eusebius says that he does not know of their being handed down as Catholic, or universally received by the Church.

The "Gospel according to Peter" is directly referred to by Origen in his Commentary on Matthew. He says: "Some say, with regard to the brethren of Jesus, from a tradition in the Gospel entitled according to Peter, or of the Book of James, that they were sons of Joseph by a former wife."14 Although this statement does not in itself necessarily favour Docetic views, it is quite intelligible that it might be used in support of them and, therefore, might have been one of the passages which excited the suspicion of Serapion, more especially as a clear statement of this family relationship is not to be found in the canonical Gospels. The part of the Gospel referred to by Origen is not, unfortunately, contained in the fragment, and consequently cannot be verified, but it is quite in accordance with its general spirit, and at least we have here a distinct mention of the Gospel without any expression of unfavourable opinion. What is more important still is the fact that Origen certainly made use of the Gospel, amongst others, himself.15

Jerome[16] likewise refers to it, after repeating the tradition that the Gospel was said to be Peter's, which Mark composed, who was his hearer and interpreter; and to the works ascribed to Peter, which Eusebius enumerates, he adds another—the "Judgment of Peter," of which little or nothing is known.

Theodoret says that the Nazarenes made use of the Gospel according to Peter.[17] Zahn and some others[18] argue against the correctness of this statement; but reasoning of this kind, based upon supposed differences of views, is not very convincing, when we consider that inferences to be drawn from peculiarities in the narrative in this Gospel are neither so distinct, nor so inevitable, as to be forced upon a simple and uncritical community, and probably that the anti-Judaistic tendency of the whole, the strongest characteristic of the composition, secured its acceptance, and diverted attention from any less marked tendencies.

A number of passages have been pointed out in the Didascalia and Apostolical Constitutions, Origen, Cyril of Jerusalem, Dionysius of Alexandria, and other ancient writers, showing the use of this Gospel according to Peter;[19] but into these later testimonies it is not necessary for us at present to go. That the work long continued to exercise considerable influence can scarcely be doubted. It is to the earlier history of the Gospel and its use in the second century that we must rather turn our attention.

A probable reference to the Gospel of Peter in Polycarp's "Epistle to the Corinthians" has been pointed out by Mr. F. C. Conybeare.[20] The writer speaks of "the testimony of the cross" (τὸ μαρτύριον τοῦ σταυροῦ), an expression which has puzzled critics a good deal. No passage in our Gospels has hitherto explained it, but if it be referred to the answer made by the cross, in our fragment, to the question from Heaven: "Hast thou preached to them that are sleeping? And an answer came from the cross, 'Yea,'" it becomes at once intelligible. Mr. Taylor[21] suggests the question whether "the word of the cross" (ὁ λόγος τοῦ σταυροῦ) in 1 Cor. i. 18 is not also connected with the same tradition of the speaking cross and, as Mr. Conybeare points out, the context favours the idea, although he himself is not inclined to admit the interpretation. The words of Paul are worth quoting:

For the word of the cross is to them that are perishing foolishness; but unto us which are being saved it is the power of God. 19. For it is written: "I will destroy the wisdom of the wise, and the prudence of the prudent will I reject;"

and so on. But although he cannot agree in the suggestion that Paul refers to this tradition, because, he says, "Such a view seems to me to be too bold and innovating in its character," Mr. Conybeare goes on to suggest that the incident in Peter, with this reply to the voice from heaven, may be

one of the "three mysteries of crying" referred to by Ignatius, ad Eph. xix. "Ritschl and Lipsius," says Lightfoot, ad locum "agree that two of the three were, (1) the voice at the baptism, (2) the voice at the transfiguration. For the third ... Ritschl supposes that Ignatius used some other Gospel containing a third proclamation similar to the two others." The Peter Gospel seems here to supply just what is wanted.[22]

These suggestions are quoted here, in dealing with Polycarp, to show that the supposition that he refers to the answer of the cross in the Gospel of Peter is not without support in other early writings. When it is remembered that the doctrine of a descent into Hell has a place in the Creed of Christendom, it is not surprising that it should be dwelt on in early writings, and that a Gospel which proclaims it by a voice from Heaven, coupled with a miraculous testimony from the cross, should be referred to. Of course it is impossible, in the absence of any explicit declaration, to establish by the passage we are discussing that the

Gospel according to Peter was used by Polycarp, but there is some probability of it at least, since no other Gospel contains the episode to which the writer seems to refer.

IV

We may now consider whether Justin Martyr was acquainted with it, and here again it may be well to remind the reader that we have only a small fragment of the Gospel according to Peter to compare with the allusions to be found in writings of the Fathers. In these early works, few quotations are made with any direct mention of the source from which they were taken, and as only those parts of Patristic writings which deal with the trial, crucifixion and resurrection of Jesus can be expected to present analogies with our fragment, it will readily be seen how limited the range of testimony must naturally be. Justin Martyr is usually supposed to have died about a.d. 163-165,[23] and his first "Apology" may be dated a.d. 147, and the "Dialogue with Trypho" somewhat later. In these writings, Justin very frequently refers to facts, and to sayings of Jesus, making, indeed, some hundred and fifty quotations of this kind from certain "Memoirs of the Apostles" (ἀπομνημονεύματα τῶν ἀποστόλων), all of which differ more or less from our present canonical Gospels. He never mentions the name of any author of these Memoirs, if indeed he was acquainted with one, unless it be upon one occasion, which is of peculiar interest in connection with our fragment. The instance to which we refer is the following. Justin says: "The statement also that he [Jesus] changed the name of Peter, one of the Apostles, and that this is written in his [Peter's] Memoirs as having been done, together with the fact that he also changed the name of other two brothers, who were sons of Zebedee, to Boanerges—that is, sons of thunder," &c.[24] It was, of course, argued that the αὐτοῦ here does not refer to Peter but to Jesus; or that the word should be amended to αὐτῶν and applied to the Apostles; but the majority of critics naturally decided against such royal ways of removing difficulties, and were forced to admit a reference to "Memoirs of Peter." Hitherto, the apologetic explanation has been that the allusion of Justin must have been to the second Synoptic, generally referred to Mark, who was held by many of the Fathers to be the mere mouthpiece and "interpreter of Peter," and that this reference is supported by the fact that the Gospel according to Mark is the only one of the four canonical works which narrates these changes of name. This argument, however, is disposed of by the fact that our second Synoptic cannot possibly be considered the work referred to in the tradition of Papias.25 Returning to Justin, we find that he designates the source of his quotations ten times as "Memoirs of the Apostles;" five times he calls it simply "Memoirs," and upon one occasion only explains that they were written "by his Apostles and their followers." He never speaks indefinitely of "Memoirs of Apostles," but always of the collective Apostles, except in the one instance which has been quoted above. In a single passage there occurs an expression which must be quoted. Justin says: "For the Apostles in the Memoirs composed by them, which are called Gospels," &c.26 The ἃ καλεῖται εὐαγγέλια has very much the appearance of a gloss in the margin of some MS., which has afterwards been transferred to the text by a scribe, as scholars have before now suggested; but in any case it makes little difference in the argument.

It is obvious that the name "Memoirs" cannot with any degree of propriety be applied to our canonical Gospels; but the discovery of this fragment, which is distinctly written as a personal narrative, throws fresh light upon the subject, and the title "Memoirs of Peter," would exactly describe the form in which the Gospel is written. It may further be suggested whether it does not give us reason for conjecturing that the earlier documents, from which our Gospels were composed, were similarly personal narratives or memoirs of those who took part in early Christian development. The tradition preserved to us by Papias distinctly points in this direction:

This also the Presbyter said: Mark having become the interpreter of Peter, wrote accurately whatever he remembered, though he did not arrange in order the things which were either said or done by Christ. For he neither heard the Lord, nor followed him; but afterwards, as I said, accompanied Peter, who adapted his teaching to the occasion, and not as making a consecutive record of the Lord's oracles.27

There can be very little doubt that the first teaching of Apostles and early catechists must have taken the form of personal recollections of various episodes of Christian history and reports of discourses and parables, with an account of the circumstances under which they were delivered. This familiar and less impressive mode of tracing Christian history must gradually have been eliminated from successive forms of the story drawn up for the use of the growing Church, until, in the Gospels adopted into the Canon, it had entirely disappeared. In the fourth Gospel, a slight trace of it remains in the reference in the third person to the writer, and it is present in parts of the Apocalypse; but a more marked instance is to be found in the "Acts of the Apostles;" not so much in the prologue—which, of course, is not really part of the book—where the author distinctly speaks in the first person, as in the narrative after the call to Macedonia (xvi. 10-17), where the writer falls into the use of the first person plural (ἡμεῖς), resumes it after a break (xx. 5-15), and abandons it again, till it is recommenced in xxi. 1-18, xxvii. 1, xxviii. 16. As the author doubtless made use of written sources of information, like the writers of our Gospels, it is most probable that, in these portions of the Acts, he simply inserted portions of personal written narratives which had come into his possession. The Gospel according to Peter, which escaped the successive revisals of the canonical Gospels, probably presents the more original form of such histories. We are, of course, unable to say whether the change of names referred to by Justin was recorded in earlier portions of this Gospel which have not been recovered, but the use of the double name, "I, Simon Peter," favours the supposition that it was.

Without attaching undue importance to it, it may be well to point out—in connection with Origen's statement that, in the Gospel according to Peter, the brethren of Jesus are represented as being of a previous marriage—that the only genealogy of Jesus which is recognised by Justin is traced through the Virgin Mary, and excludes Joseph.28 She it is who is descended from Abraham, Isaac and Jacob, and from the house of David. The genealogy of Jesus in the canonical Gospels, on the contrary, is traced solely through Joseph, who alone is stated to be of the lineage of David. The genealogies of the first and third Synoptics, though differing in several important particulars, at least agree in excluding Mary. In the third Gospel Joseph goes to Judæa "unto the city of David, which is called Bethlehem, because he was of the house and lineage of David."29 Justin simply states that Joseph went "to Bethlehem ... for his descent was from the tribe of Judah, which inhabited that region."30 Justin could not, therefore, derive his genealogies from the canonical Gospels; and his Memoirs, from which he learns the Davidic descent through Mary only, to which he refers no less than eleven times, differed from them distinctly on this point. The Gospel according to Peter, which, according to Origen, contained a statement which separated Jesus from his brethren in the flesh, in all probability must have traced the Davidic descent through Mary. The Gospel of James, commonly called the "Protevangelium," to a form of which, at least, Origen refers at the same time as the Gospel according to Peter, states that Mary was of the lineage of David.31 There are other peculiarities in Justin's account of the angelic announcement to Mary differing distinctly from our canonical Gospels,32 regarding some of which

Tischendorf was of opinion that they were derived from the "Protevangelium;" but there are reasons for supposing that they may have come from a still older work, and if it should seem that Justin made use of the Gospel according to Peter, these may also have been taken from it. In the absence of the rest of the Gospel, however, all this must be left for the present as mere conjecture.

The fragment begins with a broken sentence presenting an obviously different story of the trial of Jesus from that of the canonical Gospels. "... but of the Jews no man (τῶν δὲ Ἰουδαίων οὐδεὶς) washed his hands, neither Herod (οὐδὲ Ἡρῴδης) nor any of his judges.... Pilate rose up (ἀνέστη Πειλᾶτος). And then Herod the King (Ἡρῴδης ὁ βασιλεὺς) commandeth the Lord to be taken," &c. Justin in one place33 refers to this trial as foretold by the prophetic spirit, and speaks of what was done against the Christ "by Herod the King of the Jews, and the Jews themselves, and Pilate who was your governor among them, and his soldiers" (Ἡρῴδου τοῦ βασιλέως Ἰουδαίων καὶ αὐτῶν Ἰουδαίων καὶ Πιλάτου τοῦ ὑμετέρου παρ' αὐτοῖς γενομένου ἐπιτρόπου σὺν τοῖς αὐτοῦ στρατιώταις). This combination agrees with the representation of the fragment, and of course differs from that of the Gospels. In Dial. ciii. Justin repeats this to some extent, adding that he sent Jesus "bound" (δεδεμένον). This representation does not exist in Luke, but neither is it found in what we have of the Gospel according to Peter, though it may have occurred in the commencement of the scene to which we are so abruptly introduced.

Justin says in another place: "For as the prophet said, worrying him34 (διασύροντες αὐτὸν), they set him (ἐκάθισαν) upon a judgment seat (ἐπὶ βήματος), and said, 'Judge for us' (Κρῖνον ἡμῖν)."35 In the Gospel according to Peter we have: "They said, 'Let us drag along (σύρωμεν) the Son of God' ... and they set Him (ἐκάθισαν αὐτὸν) upon a seat of judgment (καθέδραν κρίσεως), saying, 'Judge justly (Δικαίως κρῖνε), King of Israel.' "36 This representation is different from any in our Gospels, and it has some singular points of agreement with our fragment. It has frequently been suggested that Justin, in this passage, makes use of our canonical Gospels with a combination of the Septuagint version of Isaiah lviii. 2, 3, and that this is supported by the expression "as said the prophet." This does not sufficiently explain the passage, however. The Septuagint version of the part of Isaiah lviii. 2 referred to reads: αἰτοῦσίν με νῦν κρίσιν δικαίαν—"They ask me now for just judgment."

Justin drops the "just," which stands both in Isaiah and in the fragment, and therefore the omission may be considered equally unfavourable to both writings as the source. In other respects Justin is nearer the Gospel than the prophet. On the other hand, the proposed use of καθίζειν as a transitive verb would make the fourth Gospel, xix. 13, read: "Pilate ... brought Jesus out, and set him (ἐκάθισεν) upon a judgment seat (ἐπὶ βήματος)," &c.; and it is pretended that Justin may have taken it in this sense, and that by the use of the word βῆμα he betrays his indebtedness to the fourth Gospel. This use of the verb, however, can scarcely be maintained. It is impossible to suppose that Pilate himself set Jesus on a judgment seat, as this transitive use of ἐκάθισε would require us to receive; and we must, more especially in the absence of a distinct object, receive it as the Revisers of the New Testament have rightly done—intransitively: "He brought Jesus out and sat down."37 In Justin it is not Pilate but the Jews who drag Jesus along, and put him on a judgment seat, and the use of the ordinary βῆμα for the expression of the fragment, "a seat of judgment" (καθέδρα κρίσεως), is not surprising in a writer like Justin, who is not directly quoting, but merely giving the sense of a passage. However this may be, the whole representation is peculiar, and the conclusion of many critics is that it proves Justin's dependence on the Gospel according to Peter.38

Justin, speaking of an incident of the crucifixion, says: "And those who were crucifying him parted his garments (ἐμέρισαν τὰ ἱμάτια αὐτοῦ) amongst themselves, casting lots (λαχμὸν βάλλοντες), each taking what pleased him, according to the cast of the lot (τοῦ κλήρου)."39 In the Gospel according to Peter it is said: "And they laid the clothes (τὰ ἐνδύματα) before him, and distributed them (διεμερίσαντο), and cast lots (λαχμὸν ἔβαλον) for them." The use of the peculiar expression λαχμὸν βάλλειν both by the Gospel and Justin is undoubtedly striking, especially, as Dr. Swete properly points out, as its use in this connection is limited, so far as we know, to the Gospel of Peter, Justin, and Cyril.40 It is rendered more important by the fact that, both in the Gospel and Justin, the casting of lots is applied to all the clothes, in contradistinction to the fourth Gospel, in which it is connected with the coat alone, and that neither has any mention of the Johannine peculiarity that the coat was without seam.

Justin says that after he was crucified all the "acquaintances of Jesus forsook him" (οἱ γνώριμοι αὐτοῦ πάντες ἀπέστησαν);41 and in another place that after his crucifixion "the disciples who were with him dispersed (διεσκεδάσθησαν) until he rose from the dead."42 This representation is found in the first Synoptic only, but agrees still better with vv. 26, 27, and 59 of our fragment. Elsewhere, Justin, in agreement with the fragment, speaks of Herod, "King of the Jews."43 Further, he says, more than once, that the Jews sent persons throughout the world to spread calumnies against Christians, amongst which was the story that "his disciples stole him by night from the grave (κλέψαντες αὐτὸν ἀπὸ τοῦ μνήματος νυκτός) where he had been laid when he was unloosed from the cross (ἀφηλωθεὶς ἀπὸ τοῦ σταυροῦ)."44 The first Synoptic alone has the expression regarding the disciples stealing the body, using the same verb, but our fragment alone uses μνῆμα for the tomb and offers a parallel for the unloosing from the cross in v. 21. We must, however, point out that the statement regarding these emissaries from the Jews is not found at all in our canonical Gospels.45

It will be remembered that, in the fragment, the only cry from the cross is: " 'Power, my Power, thou hast forsaken me,' and having spoken, he was taken up." This is one of the most striking variations from the canonical Gospels. It is also claimed as, perhaps, the most Docetic representation of the fragment, for the idea was that one Christ suffered and rose, and another flew up and was free from suffering.46 It was believed by the Docetae that the Holy Spirit only descended upon the human Jesus, at his baptism, in the shape of a dove. Now one of the statements of Justin from his Memoirs, which has no existence in our Gospels, was that, when Jesus went to be baptized by John,

As Jesus went down to the water, a fire was also kindled in the Jordan; and when he came up from the water, the Holy Spirit like a dove fell upon him, as the Apostles of this very Christ of ours wrote ... and at the same time a voice came from the heavens ... "Thou art my son, this day have I begotten thee."
Justin repeats his version of the words a second time in the same chapter.47 The Synoptics make the voice say: "Thou art my beloved son; in thee I am well pleased," instead of the words from Psalm ii. 7. Now, although we have not the part of the Gospel according to Peter in which the earlier history of Jesus is related, it is not improbable that Justin's version, agreeing as it does with the later episode in the fragment and with the criticism of Serapion, was taken from this Gospel.

We refer to this point, however, for the purpose of introducing another statement of Justin, which may be worth a little consideration in connection with our fragment. One of the passages which are supposed most clearly to betray Docetic tendencies is the expression, v. 10, that when the Lord was crucified "he kept silence, as feeling no pain" (ὡς μηδὲν πόνον ἔχων). It is evident that these words may either be taken as simply representing the fortitude with which suffering was endured, or understood to support the view that no pain was really suffered, though this is by no means actually said. Now, Justin, in another chapter of his "Dialogue with Trypho," in which he again refers to the baptism and quotes the words of the voice as above, cites the agony in the garden to prove that "the Father wished his Son really to suffer (πάθεσιν ἀληθῶς) for our sakes, and that we may not say that he, being the Son of God, did not feel what was happening and being inflicted upon him."48 He goes on to say that the silence of Jesus, who returned no answer to any one in the presence of Pilate, was foretold in a passage which he quotes. All this, in connection with representations not found in our canonical Gospels, may form another link with the Gospel according to Peter, as one of his Memoirs. Justin evidently made use of passages like the words at the baptism, to which he did not attach any Docetic interpretation, and it is quite natural that he should argue against the view that Jesus did not really suffer pain, and yet read quite naturally the words we are discussing, without directly referring to them. It was the practice of these early sects to twist passages, not originally intended to favour them, into evidence for their views, and an ordinary Christian might possess a Gospel containing them, in complete unconsciousness that it tended in the slightest degree to encourage heresy.49 It is evident from several quotations which we have made, and from others which might be adduced, that Justin was an example of this very thing.

A number of small points might be added to these, but we do not go into them here. A majority of the critics who have discussed the question are of opinion that Justin made use of the Gospel according to Peter,50 and even apologists, (who as a body seem agreed to depreciate the fragment), whilst refusing to admit its use by Justin, are not generally very decided in their denial nor, as we shall presently see, inclined to assign it a date which excludes the possibility. The case may be summed up in a few words. Justin undeniably quotes from his "Memoirs of the Apostles" facts and passages which are not found in our Gospels; he distinctly refers to statements as contained in certain "Memoirs of Peter;"51 some of these variations from the canonical Gospels have linguistic and other parallels in our fragment, short as it is, and there is reason to suppose that others would have been found in it had the entire Gospel been extant for comparison; the style of the fragment precisely tallies with the peculiar name of "Memoirs," being a personal narrative in the first person singular; and finally, there is nothing in its composition or character which necessitates the assignment of such a date to the fragment as would exclude the possibility, or probability, of its use by Justin.

V

We may now consider whether there is any indication of the use of this Gospel according to Peter by the author of the "Epistle of Barnabas." The Epistle is variously dated between a.d. 70-132, apologists leaning towards the earlier date. The shortness of the fragment recovered, of course, diminishes greatly the probability of finding any trace of its use in so comparatively brief a work as this Epistle, but some indications may be pointed out. The fragment states that, being anxious lest the sun should set whilst he was still living and the law regarding one put to death be transgressed, "one of them said: 'Give him to drink gall with vinegar,' and having mixed they gave him to drink (Ποτίσατε αὐτὸν χολὴν μετὰ ὄξους· καὶ κεράσαντες ἐπότισαν).52 ... Over all these things, however, we were fasting (ἐπὶ δὲ τούτοις πᾶσιν ἐνηστεύομεν)53 ... the whole people ... beat their breasts (ὁ λαὸς ἅπας ... κόπτεται τὰ στήθη)."54 This representation not only differs from the canonical Gospels in "gall with vinegar" being given to drink, but in the view that it was not given to relieve thirst, but as a potion to hasten death,55 and there follow various statements regarding fasting and mourning. Now in Barnabas precisely the same representation is made. The Epistle says:

But also when crucified, he had vinegar and gall given him to drink (ἀλλὰ καὶ σταυρωθεὶς ἐποτίζετο ὄξει καὶ χολῇ). Hear how, on this matter, the priests of the temple have revealed. Seeing that there is a commandment in Scripture: "Whosoever shall not observe the fast shall surely die," the Lord commanded, because he was in his own person about to offer the vessel of his spirit for our sins ... "Since ye are to give me, who am to offer my flesh for the sins of my new people, gall with vinegar to drink, eat ye alone, while the people fasts and wails.... (μέλλετε ποτίζειν χολὴν μετὰ ὄξους ... τοῦ λαοῦ νηστεύοντος καὶ κοπτομένου)."56

There are three suppositions as the possible explanation of this similarity: (1) that the author of the Epistle derived his statement from the Gospel; (2) that the author of the Gospel derived it from the Epistle, or (3) that both drew it from a third and earlier source. Assigning as we do the later date to the Epistle of Barnabas, the first of these hypotheses seems to us the most natural and the correct one, although, of course, it is impossible to prove that both did not derive it from another source. The second explanation we must definitely reject, both because we consider that priority of date lies with the fragment, and because it does not seem probable that the representation originated in the Epistle. To admit this would be to suppose that the author first fabricated the statement that Jesus was given gall and vinegar to hasten death, and then proceeded immediately to explain the circumstance by means of the elaborate gnosis with which the Epistle is filled. It is quite undeniable that the whole narrative of the Gospels grew out of the suggestions of supposed prophetic passages in the Old Testament, but the author of the Epistle introduces the statement upon which his explanation is based, with a simplicity which seems to exclude the idea of its being his own fabrication: "But also, when crucified, he had vinegar and gall given him to drink." There is not the ring here of a statement advanced for the first time, but if we suppose that the author had read it in such a work as the Gospel according to Peter, it would be quite natural. It is not to be understood that we doubt that the account in the fragment, or in our Gospels, was suggested by passages in the Old Testament, but simply that we do not believe that the representation originated in this Epistle, in immediate connection with the elaborate explanation given. A tradition, gradually influenced by such prophetic and other considerations, may have been embodied by the author of the Gospel in his narrative, and then the writer of the Epistle may have seized upon it and enlarged upon its typical signification, but it is not probable that he originated it himself.

VI

We do not propose to enter here upon an inquiry whether there is any evidence within our short fragment that the Gospel according to Peter was used by other early writers. The slight traces which alone we could hope to find, and which several able critics do find,57 cannot be decisive of anything, and whilst there may be a faint literary interest in pursuing such researches, they need not detain us here. A short consideration may, however, be given to Tatian. Some critics, impressed apparently with the idea that no early Gospels can possibly be otherwise than dependent on our canonical works, yet having to explain the continuous divergence from the canonical narratives, advance the suggestion, that the writer of the Gospel according to Peter may have derived all the points which the fragment contains, in common with one or more of the canonical Gospels, from a Harmony of our Gospels. Now, the only Harmony of the second century which, they think, has survived is the so-called "Diatessaron" of Tatian. Of course, they find that the "Diatessaron" "might have furnished the writer of the fragment with all the incidents which he shares with any of the Four Gospels." Dr. Swete continues: "The order in Peter is not always the same as it seems to have been in Tatian, but differences of order may be disregarded in our inquiry, since they are equally embarrassing if we assume that the writer had recourse to the Gospels as separate books."58

Not content with the conclusion that the Gospels, narrating the very same history, might have furnished the incidents which they have in common, Dr. Swete proceeds "to compare the 'Diatessaron' with our fragment, with the view of ascertaining whether Tatian would have provided the Petrine writer with the words which he seems to have adopted from the Four Gospels."59

This is not the place to discuss again the identity of the supposed "Diatessaron," but it will be sufficient to point out that we have it only in an Arabic version, published and translated by Ciasca, and a translation of the supposed Armenian version of the Commentary upon it, ascribed to Ephraem, which again Moesinger, who edited the Latin version published in 1876, declares to be itself translated from the Syriac. In these varied transformations of the text, anything like verbal accuracy must be regarded as totally lost. The object in making the versions was not, of course, critical fidelity, and variations from canonical texts would, no doubt, often or always be regarded as accidental and to be corrected. Such translations can never, in textual criticism, be accepted as sufficient representations of the original. The process, however, by which Dr. Swete proceeds to ascertain whether the author of the fragment derives from Tatian the words which he seems to have adopted from the Four Gospels, is to place side by side with the Petrine narrative, in certain crucial passages, the corresponding portions of the "Diatessaron," approximately represented in Greek, and he selects the accounts of the mockery, the three hours, the burial, and the visit of the women to the tomb. He thus explains his system: "The plan adopted has been to substitute for Ciasca's translation of the Arabic Tatian the corresponding portions of the canonical Gospels. The text has been determined by a comparison of Ciasca's Latin with Moesinger's Evangelii Concordantis Expositio, and the Curetonian Syriac of Luke xxiii., xxiv. It claims, of course, only to be an approximate and provisional representation of the text of the original work."60 However impartial Dr. Swete may have tried to be—and without doubt he did endeavour to be so—such a test is vitiated and rendered useless by the antecedent manipulation of the texts. The result at which he arrives is: "This comparison does not justify the conclusion that the writer of our fragment was limited to the use of the 'Diatessaron' "—the exact contents of which, in its original shape, be it noted, Dr. Swete, a few lines further on, admits that we do not know, "so that it would be unsafe to draw any negative inference" from certain exceptions.

On the whole we may perhaps claim to have established a strong presumption that the Petrine writer employed a Harmony which, in its general selection of extracts, and in some of its minuter arrangements, very nearly resembled the Harmony of Tatian. This is not equivalent to saying that he used Tatian, because there is some reason to think that there may have been a Harmony or Harmonies earlier than Tatian.... Thus the relation of the Petrine writer to Tatian remains for the present an open question; but enough has been said to render such a relation probable, if further inquiries should lead us to place the Gospel of Peter after the publication of the "Diatessaron."61
It must frankly be asserted that the whole of this comparison with Tatian, and the views so curiously expressed regarding the result, are the outcome of a preconceived idea that the Petrine

author compiled his Gospel mainly from the canonical. The divergencies being so great, however, and the actual contradictions so strong, it becomes necessary to account for them in some way, and the theory of the use of a Harmony is advanced to see whether it may not overcome some of the difficulties. It would have been more to the purpose to have inquired whether the so-called "Diatessaron" did not make use of the Gospel according to Peter, amongst others.

In connection with this it may be well to refer to some remarkable observations of Professor J. Rendel Harris regarding the relation of the Gospel according to Peter and Tatian's Harmony. When the fragment was first discovered, he was naturally struck by its great importance. "The Gospel of Peter, even in the imperfect form in which it has come down to us, is the breaking of a new seal, the opening of a fresh door," he said, "to those who are engaged in the problems presented by Biblical and Patristic criticism,"62 and he very rightly proceeded to try to find out "whether Peter has used Tatian, or Tatian Peter, or whether both of them are working upon common sources."63 He first refers to "a curious addition to the story of the Crucifixion, which can be shown, with a very high probability, to have once stood in the Harmony of Tatian." The most interesting and instructive part of the reference is that Mr. Harris had made and published, some years before the discovery of the fragment before us, certain notes on the Harmony of Tatian, in which he had employed "the method of combination of passages in different writers who were known to have used the Harmony, or different texts which were suspected of having borrowed from it, to show that in the account of the Crucifixion there stood a passage something like the following:

"They beat their breasts and said, Woe unto us, for the things which are done to-day for our sins; for the desolation of Jerusalem hath drawn nigh."64

It is unnecessary here to quote the way Mr. Harris arrived at this passage, which he frankly states, but at once go on to compare it with our fragment. He sums up:

Now the reader will be interested to see that the missing sentence which I restored to Tatian's text has turned up in the Gospel of Peter, for we read that: "The Jews and the elders and the priests, when they saw what an evil deed they had done to themselves, began to beat their breasts and to say, Woe to our sins, for the judgment and the end of Jerusalem is at hand." Did the false Peter take this from Tatian, or was it the other way? or did both of them use some uncanonical writing or tradition?65 "There is nothing in what follows in the Arabic Harmony," Mr. Harris points out, "which suggests an allusion to the desolation of the city, or an imprecation upon, or lamentation over, themselves."66

Very few will feel any doubt that this is taken from our Gospel according to Peter, or possibly—for of course there is no absolute proof—from the tradition which the writer of that Gospel also used, and not by the writer from the Harmony; and it may be suggested that the omission of this and similar passages from versions of the Harmony may have been influenced by the fact that, not forming part of our Gospels, and not agreeing with the preconceived theory of a Harmony of our four Gospels, such passages were excluded as interpolations.

Another instance given by Mr. Harris is the statement in the fragment: "Then the sun shone out, and it was found to be the ninth hour," which he compares with the language of "Tatian's" commentator: "Three hours the sun was darkened, and afterwards it shone out again."67 And further:

Another case of parallelism is in the speech of the angel to Mary: "He is not here, for he is risen, and has gone away to the place from whence he was sent." At first sight this looks like a wilful expansion on the part of the writer of the Gospel; but on a reference to the Persian father Aphrahat, who is more than suspected of having used the text of Tatian, we find the words, "And the angels said to Mary, He is risen, and gone away to him that sent him," which is very nearly in coincidence with the text of the false Peter.68

Neither of these passages is found in the actual text of "Tatian." Finally, we may quote the other instance pointed out by Mr. Harris:

The Docetic quotation from the Psalm "My Power, my Power, hast thou forsaken me?" is peculiar in this respect, that the second possessive pronoun is wanting, so that we ought to translate it "Power, my Power ..." Now, it is curious that Tatian's text had a similar peculiarity, for Ephrem gives it as "God, my God," and the Arabic Harmony as Yaiil, Yaiili, where the added suffix belongs to the possessive pronoun. This is a remarkable coincidence, and makes one suspect that Tatian had "Power, my Power" in his text, and that it has been corrected away. And it is significant that Ephrem in commenting on the passage, says: "The divinity did not so far depart from the humanity as to be cut off from it, but only as regards the power of the divinity, which was hidden both from the Slain and the slayers." This looks very suspicious that Ephrem found something in his text of Tatian differing from the words "God, my God."69

Mr. Harris reserves his final judgment on this relation between Tatian and the Gospel according to Peter; but as in a later article70 he is not unwilling to allow the date of a.d. 130 to be assigned to the fragment, it is scarcely to be decided as Peter quoting Tatian. Mr. Harris throughout these passages, however, states the case in a most impartial manner, and the reader must form his own opinion.

We may, before leaving "Tatian," point out another instance of agreement to which Mr. Harris does not allude. In the Commentary there is the following passage: "Et dederunt ei bibere acetum et fel. Acetum ei porrexerunt, pro felle autem magna ejus miseratio amaritudinem gentium dulcem fecit."71 It will be remembered that this agrees with the representation of the fragment that they gave Jesus "vinegar and gall" to drink.

All these instances may, indeed, throw a new light upon the Diapente in the text of Victor, which has so exercised apologists, and lead to the opinion that Tatian's Harmony was not composed out of four Gospels, but out of five. If it be agreed, as it is by a majority of critics, that Justin made use of the Gospel of Peter, the probability that his pupil Tatian likewise possessed the same work, and used it for his Harmony, is immensely increased.

VII

We shall not attempt to fix any even approximate date to the Gospel according to Peter, although we shall presently have to consider its relation to our canonical Gospels in a way which will at least assign it a position in time relative to them. Harnack, in the preface to the second edition of his article on the fragment, suspends his judgment on its relation to our Gospels, and will not even undertake a sufficient examination of this important question, so long as there remains a hope of still recovering more of the Gospel. It is devoutly to be hoped that the Cemetery of Akhmîm may still give us more of this and other important early works; but there is no reason why we should not, even now, endeavour to derive what information we can from this instalment, and the worst—or the best—which can happen is that future acquisitions may enable us to correct the errors—or confirm the conclusions—of the present. So long as we confine ourselves to the legitimate inferences to be drawn from the actual fragment before us, we cannot go far wrong.

It is frequently possible to assign well-defined limits within which early works, whose authors are unknown, must have been composed, when a more precise date cannot with certainty be fixed. Direct references to the writing, or its use, by writers the period of whose literary work is known, may enable us to affirm that it was written at least before their time; and sometimes certain allusions or quotations in the work itself may, on the other hand, show that it must have been composed after a certain date; and thus limits, more or less narrow, become certain, within which its production must lie. The Gospel according to Peter, as we might expect, contains none of the allusions or quotations to which we refer, and we are therefore reduced to the one indication of age—reference to, or the use of it by, early writers, leaving the approximate date to which it may be set back wholly to conjecture. As we have already remarked above, the question whether it is dependent on, or independent of, our canonical Gospels has yet to be considered; but there is too much difference of opinion regarding the date of these Gospels themselves to render this more than a relative indication. So far, the opinions of critics assign the Gospel according to Peter to dates ranging from a period antecedent to our Gospels, in their present form, to about the middle of the second century.72

The indications of style and phraseology given by the fragment have of course to be taken into account, and it may be well, before proceeding further, to examine certain peculiarities which have been pointed out by writers who assert that the composition is decidedly later than our canonical Gospels.73 The writer never speaks of "Jesus" simply, but always as "the Lord" (ὁ κύριος). He likewise refers to him as the "Saviour" (σωτήρ) in one place, and several times as "a Son of God" (υἱὸς τοῦ θεοῦ).

Now, with regard to these expressions, they are in constant use throughout the New Testament writings, in the Gospels themselves, as well as in the Epistles of Paul and the Epistles popularly ascribed to him. For instance, ὁ κύριος: Matt. xxi. 3, xxviii. 6;74 Mark xvi. 19;75 Luke vii. 13, x. 1, xi. 39, xii. 42, xiii. 15, xvii. 5, 6, xviii. 6, xix. 8, 31, 34, xxii. 61, xxiv. 3, 34; John vi. 23, xi. 2, xiii. 13, 14, xx. 2, 13, 18, 20, 28, xxi. 7, 12. It is unnecessary to point out passages in the Acts and Epistles, for "the Lord," "the Lord Jesus," or "the Lord Jesus Christ," is everywhere used, and indeed no other form, it may be said, is adopted. "A Son of God" (υἱὸς τοῦ θεοῦ) is constantly used in the Gospels and Acts. A few instances may be given: Matt. viii. 29, xiv. 33, xvi. 16, xxvi. 63, xxvii. 40, 43, 54; Mark i. 1, iii. 11, v. 7, xv. 39; Luke i. 35, ix. 41, viii. 28, xxii. 70; John i. 34, 49, v. 25, x. 36, xi. 4, 27, xix. 7, xx. 31; Acts ix. 20. Of course, in the Epistles the expression is of frequent occurrence, as for instance, Rom. i. 4, 9, v. 10; 1 Cor. i. 9; 2 Cor. i. 19; Gal. ii. 20, and elsewhere. It is not necessary to show that "Saviour" is used, but the following may be pointed out: Luke ii. 11; John iv. 42; Acts v. 31, xiii. 23; and it more frequently occurs in the Epistles. All of these expressions are commonly employed in early Christian literature, such as the "Didache," Ignatian Epistles, Clement of Rome, Polycarp, "Pastor" of Hermas, and the "Apology" of Aristides.

The principal phrase upon which weight is laid by those who assign to the Gospel according to Peter, from this fragment, a later date than our canonical works, is the use of ἡ κυριακή without ἡμέρα to designate "the Lord's day"—Sunday; Dr. Swete calls it "the most decisive indication of the relatively late composition of our fragment."76 After giving some instances of a similar expression, he states the case as follows:

The name was therefore familiar amongst Eastern Greek-speaking Christians from the end of the first century. But Peter not only uses it freely, but seems to be unconscious that he is guilty of an anachronism when he imports this exclusively Christian term into the Gospel history. Ἡ κυριακή has so completely supplanted Ἡ μία τῶν σαββάτων, that it is twice used to describe the first Easter Day, in a document which usually manifests precision in such matters.77

It is not quite clear what Dr. Swete means when he says that Peter "uses it freely," but it would indeed be singular if he seemed to be conscious that he was guilty of an anachronism in making use of this or any word. The question, in fact, is whether it is an anachronism or not, and that it is so is very far from proved by any arguments yet brought forward. In the Apocalypse, i. 10, we have the use of the term "the Lord's day" (ἡ κυριακὴ ἡμέρα), a.d. 68-69. In the "Didache," which Dr. Lightfoot assigns to the first or the beginning of the second century, we meet with κυριακὴ κυρίου; and in the Ignatian Epistles, which those who believe in them date "in the early years of the second century," there is in one place78 κατὰ κυριακήν. So far from its being surprising that there should not be more authority for such an expression, however, it seems almost more remarkable that we should have any parallels at all, when we remember how few early writings are extant, and how few of these actually refer to the day thus designated. The Epistles, for this reason, may be set aside in a body, for they give no testimony either way, with the exception of 1 Cor. xvi. 2, where "the first day of the week" is referred to. The three Synoptics, following each other, and a common tradition, use ἡ μία τῶν σαββάτων each once, and the fourth Gospel has the same phrase twice, and the Acts once; but this use of another expression does not—in the face of the use of ἡ κυριακή in this fragment, and of ἡ κυριακὴ ἡμέρα, in the Apocalypse—at all show that, at the same period, the latter phrase was not also current, though it may not have supplanted "the first day of the week." The fact that Melito of Sardis, "about the middle of the second century," wrote a treatise περὶ κυριακῆς shows how general that expression had become; and even Dr. Swete, as we have seen above, recognises that it was "familiar amongst Eastern Greek-speaking Christians from the end of the first century." There is nothing whatever to warrant the conclusion that its use at the time when our Gospels were written would have been an anachronism, but the fact that a different expression happened to be used in a few writings. The author of the fragment employs the phrase twice only, and it is thoroughly consistent with his impressive style throughout the episode, that he should apply to the time when these astounding events are said to have taken place the appropriate term, already suggested by the author of the Apocalypse, of "the Lord's day," instead of "the first day of the week." There is nothing more difficult, as is proved every day in our time, than to fix the precise date at which words or expressions first came into use, and especially—in the absence of voluminous literature opposing the presumption—the denial of antiquity to a work, on the ground of its employing an expression supposed only to have come into general use a few years later than its otherwise probable date, is both rash and unjustifiable.

VIII

We now come to the most important part of our examination of this fragment, whether in regard to its approximate date or to its intrinsic value as an early Christian document—its relation to our canonical Gospels. The fragment begins and ends with a broken sentence, but taking it as it stands, in comparison with the same episodes in our four canonical Gospels, it contains about a fourth more matter. It will be seen that it is very far from a Harmony of the four narratives, and still less an abridgment of their common tradition, but it has markedly the character of an independent history drawn from similar, but varying, sources.

The fragment commences, "but of the Jews no man washed his hands, neither Herod nor any of his judges; and as they were not minded to wash, Pilate rose.79 (2) And then Herod the King commandeth the Lord to be taken, saying unto them: 'Whatsoever I commanded that ye should do, that do unto him.'" It is clear from this that the tribunal before which it is represented that Jesus was taken for trial was quite different from that described in the canonical Gospels. Herod and other Jewish judges must, according to the writer, have sat along with Pilate, but the order given by "Herod the King" "to take the Lord" evidently shows that he is represented as playing the leading part. Although the episode of the washing of the hands (of which so much more is made by the author of the first Synoptic, who alone of the canonical Evangelists refers to it) must have been introduced, we have no means of knowing how far the two accounts may have agreed. Both, at least in one shape or another, adopt a tradition so incredible as that representing a Roman governor coerced into condemning an innocent man, and helplessly going through such a ceremony for the purpose of clearing himself from responsibility for gross injustice. The third Synoptist is the only one of the canonical Evangelists who prominently brings forward the share of Herod in judging Jesus (xxiii. 6-15), and he is in curious agreement with the spirit of Peter's account when he represents Pilate (xxiii. 6-7), on hearing that Jesus was a Galilean, recognising "that he was of Herod's jurisdiction," and sending him to Herod, "who himself also was at Jerusalem in these days." The statement also (xxiii. 12) that Herod and Pilate, having before been at enmity, became friends that day through this very act recognising Herod's jurisdiction, seems to point to a tradition coupling Herod with the trial, a form of which we have in the fragment. All the other Gospels are not only silent upon the point, but exclude his participation in the matter. When, according to our fragment, "Pilate rose," he seems to have passed out of all connection with the trial and condemnation of Jesus.

At this point, Peter represents the request for the body of Jesus as having been made but, before considering this part of his narrative, we must note the portions of the canonical account which he altogether omits. The first of these to which we must refer is the preference of Barabbas, which all of our four Evangelists carefully relate. Considering that his main object in writing this Gospel, according to some critics, was animosity to the Jews and a desire to cast upon them the whole guilt and responsibility of the death of Jesus, it is very remarkable that he should altogether exclude this picturesque episode, and sacrifice so favourable an opportunity of throwing upon them the odium of crying "Not this man, but Barabbas." There is strong presumptive evidence here of his entire independence of our four Gospels, for it is not reasonable to suppose that, if he had them before him, he could deliberately have passed over such striking material. A further indication of the same kind is to be found in the fact that he apparently knows nothing of the appeals made by Pilate to the people in favour of Jesus, so furiously rejected by them. It is distinctly a merit in the narrative of Peter that he does not, like the four Evangelists, give us the very extraordinary spectacle of a Roman Governor and Judge feebly expostulating with a noisy Jewish mob in favour of an accused person brought for trial before him, whom he repeatedly declares to be innocent, and at last allowing himself to be coerced against his will into scourging and crucifying him.

According to the four canonical Gospels,[80] the request of Joseph for the body of Jesus is made after he has expired on the cross. In Matthew (xxvii. 57 f.) he is a rich man from Arimathaea named Joseph, who also himself was a disciple of Jesus, and he goes to Pilate and asks for the body, which Pilate commands to be given to him. In Mark (xv. 43) Joseph of Arimathaea, a councillor of honourable estate, who also himself was looking for the kingdom of God, boldly goes in unto Pilate and asks for the body of Jesus. According to Matthew it is "When even was come" that he goes to Pilate; in Mark it is "When even was now come, because it was the Preparation, that is, the day before the Sabbath." In Matthew, Pilate simply commands that the body should be given; but in Mark it is further related (xv. 44): "And Pilate marvelled if he were already dead: and calling unto him the centurion, he asked him whether he had been any while dead. And when he learned it of the centurion he granted the corpse to Joseph." In Luke (xxiii. 50 f.): "A man named Joseph, who was a councillor, a good man and a righteous (he had not consented to their counsel and deed), of Arimathaea, a city of the Jews, who was looking for the kingdom of God: this man went to Pilate and asked for the body of Jesus." It is implied, but not said, that it was granted, and the time is mentioned further on (v. 54): "And it was the day of the Preparation, and the Sabbath drew on,"—which recalls Mark. In John (xix. 38): "After these things [the crurifragium and piercing of the side], Joseph of Arimathaea, being a disciple of Jesus, but secretly for fear of the Jews, asked of Pilate that he might take away the body of Jesus: and Pilate gave him leave." In Peter, the request is made before Jesus is actually sent to be crucified, and the author is sometimes accused of perverting the narrative by introducing it at this time. It is impossible to see any object for so altering the sequence of events as given by the four canonical Gospels, on the supposition that he knew them, and it will be seen that the time in Peter's narrative is in perfect accord with the version which he gives of the trial. "Pilate rose," and it is to be inferred that he left the Praetorium. It is at this moment that Joseph seizes the opportunity of asking for the body: 3. "But there was there Joseph the friend of Pilate[81] and of the Lord, and knowing that they are about to crucify (σταυρίσκειν) him, he came to Pilate and asked the body of the Lord for burial. 4. And Pilate sent to Herod and asked for his body; 5. and Herod said: 'Brother Pilate, even if no one had begged for him, we should have buried him, because the Sabbath is at hand, for it is written in the Law: The sun must not go down upon one put to death.'" It is to be noted that, whilst in the four canonical Gospels the request for the body is immediately followed by the entombment, in our fragment the request is made in anticipation, when a favourable moment for the request presented itself, and the actual reception of the body follows later, in its proper place. It is possible that the statement, in Luke (xxiii. 50-51), that Joseph was "a councillor" who had "not consented to their counsel and deed," which is here alone referred to, may indicate another tradition, of part of which Peter may have availed himself, and that it included his presence at the trial and consequently presented the opportunity of at once going to Pilate. That Pilate should send on the request to Herod is only in keeping with the representation that he had withdrawn from the trial, and would not himself further interfere in the matter. The mode of carrying on his narrative, by direct utterances put into the mouths of his personages, is particularly characteristic of the writer, and forms a remarkable feature of his style throughout. There is no sign of dependence upon the canonical Gospels in all this: but, on the contrary, the almost complete departure from their representations, in order and in substance, is only explicable on the hypothesis of a separate, though analogous, tradition.

If we look at the language, we find that critics point out one phrase which is common to the three Synoptics: "He went in unto Pilate [and] asked for the body of Jesus" (προσελθὼν τῷ Πειλάτῳ ᾐτήσατο τὸ σῶμα τοῦ Ἰησοῦ,82 Matthew and Luke; εἰσῆλθεν πρὸς τὸν Πειλᾶτον καὶ ᾐτήσατο τὸ σῶμα τοῦ Ἰησοῦ, Mark). In Peter we have: "He came to Pilate and asked for the body of the Lord" (ἦλθεν πρὸς τὸν Πειλᾶτον καὶ ᾔτησε τὸ σῶμα τοῦ κυρίου). It will be observed that the language of the three Synoptists is almost exactly the same, and although their interdependence throughout requires another explanation, which need not be entered into here, it is quite unreasonable to infer dependence on the part of Peter from similarity in these few words. It is the description of a perfectly simple action, in the most simple and natural language, and it is difficult to imagine what other words could be used without inflation. All the rest of the episode differs in every respect of language, order and substantial detail. It is right to add, however, that no great weight is attached by anyone to the point. On the other hand, it may be pointed out that σταυρίσκειν, in Peter, is a most uncommon word, not used in the New Testament at all, and that ταφή only occurs once in the New Testament, in Matt. xxvii. 7.

The fragment continues:

And he delivered him to the people before the first day of the Unleavened bread of their feast (πρὸ μιᾶς τῶν ἀζύμων, τῆς ἑορτῆς αὐτῶν). 6. And taking the Lord they pushed him hurrying along, and said: "Let us drag along (σύρωμεν) the Son of God as we have power over him." 7. And they clad him with purple (πορφύραν αὐτὸν περιέβαλλον) and set him on a seat of judgment (καθέδραν κρίσεως), saying: "Judge justly (δικαίως κρῖνε), King of Israel." 8. And one of them brought a crown of thorns and set it upon the head of the Lord. 9. And others standing by spat in his eyes, and others smote him on the cheeks; others pierced him with a reed, and some scourged him, saying: "With this honour honour we the Son of God."

Before proceeding to compare this passage with our Gospels, it may be well to determine who the mockers in this fragment really are. It is argued by Zahn[83] and others, that Herod, according to this representation, hands Jesus over to the Jews, and that the people, and not the soldiers, as in the Gospels, conduct the mockery which is here described. It cannot be denied that the words used are, "he delivered him to the people" (παρέδωκεν αὐτὸν τῷ λαῷ), but the question is, whether the meaning is that he actually delivered him into the hands of the mob, and that the subsequent mockery, scourging, crucifixion and parting of the garments were performed by the people, or that, in delivering Jesus to the people, the meaning is not rather that he gave him up to their demands that he should be crucified, and that all the rest followed between soldiers and people, as in the other narratives. We cannot but affirm that this latter interpretation is the true one. In Luke (xxiii. 25) the form of words used exactly expresses this: "but Jesus he delivered up to their will" (τὸν δὲ Ἰησοῦν παρέδωκεν τῷ θελήματι αὐτῶν). But a still more close representation of the case occurs in the fourth Gospel, where we read (xix. 16 f.): "Then, therefore, he delivered him unto them [the people and the chief priests] to be crucified. They took Jesus, therefore ... unto the place called, &c. ... where they crucified him." It is only in verse 23 that the narrative goes back and explains: "The soldiers, therefore, when they had crucified Jesus," &c. In the fragment, moreover, there is an important indication in the portion previously quoted, where we read: 2. "And then Herod the King commandeth the Lord to be taken, saying unto them: 'Whatsoever I commanded that ye should do, that do unto him.' " Who are indicated by the pronoun "them"?84 Doubtless the context would have explained this and probably made clear all that follows, for the orders given must have been regarding the crucifixion, since in the following verse (3) it is said that Joseph, "knowing that they are about to crucify him," came to Pilate. Nothing had previously been said, in this fragment, of crucifixion. It is not possible to admit that the writer intends to represent that the people themselves carried out the crucifixion, or that the orders given by Herod were to the crowd. Herod, in all probability, is represented as commanding his own soldiers, which would accord with the statement in the third Synoptic (xxiii. 11), that Herod "with his soldiers set him at nought and mocked him," and so on. The doubt only proceeds from indefinite statement on the part of the writer, and preconceived ideas on the part of critics.

It is evident, from the statement that Jesus was delivered for crucifixion "before the first day of the Unleavened bread of their feast," that the Gospel of Peter adopts the same chronology as the fourth Gospel, in contradiction to that of the three Synoptics, and represents Jesus as put to death on the 14th Nisan. His agreement with the fourth Gospel, however, is limited to the mere matter of date, for on all other points the author takes a widely different view. As Hilgenfeld points out, for him all the feasts prescribed by the Law are mere Jewish institutions, and he has none of the Johannine (xix. 33 f.) views as to the death of Jesus representing the Paschal offering, nor does he associate with that the circumstances regarding the breaking of the limbs, and the thrust of the spear in his side, which he altogether omits.85

The author of the fragment is reproached with the looseness of his narrative of the mockery, on the supposition that he represents the clothing in purple and the setting on the seat of judgment as occurring whilst Jesus is being dragged along by the Jews; but this is not the case. The hurrying along commences the mockery in verse 6. Then in verse 7 begins another episode. They clothe Jesus in purple and set him on the judgment seat. Now, before going into the details of this mockery, it is necessary to consider how the narrative in general accords with the account in the four canonical Gospels. In Peter, the whole of the mockery is represented as taking place after Jesus is delivered to be crucified. He is hustled along, clothed in purple and set upon a seat of judgment; the crown of thorns is put upon his head, they spit in his eyes and smite him on the cheeks, pierce him with a reed and scourge him. In the Synoptics, especially, the ill-usage is as much as possible lengthened and intensified. In Matthew, the mockery begins when Jesus is in the house of Caiaphas (xxvi. 67 f.): "Then did they spit in his face and buffet him; and some smote him with the palms of their hands, saying, Prophesy unto us, thou Christ: who is he that struck thee?" After Pilate causes Jesus to be scourged, and delivers him, the mockery begins afresh (xxvii. 27 ff.): "Then the soldiers of the governor took Jesus into the Palace and gathered unto him the whole band. And they stripped him, and put on him a scarlet robe. And they plaited a crown of thorns and put it upon his head, and a reed in his right hand; and they kneeled down before him and mocked him, saying, Hail, King of the Jews! And they spat upon him and took the reed and smote him on the head. And when they had mocked him they took off from him the robe and put on him his garments, and led him away to crucify him." In Mark, the mockery also begins in the house of the high priest (xiv. 65 ff.): "And some began to spit on him, and to cover his face and to buffet him, and to say unto him: Prophesy: and the officers received him with blows of their hands." The mockery recommences after Jesus is scourged and delivered over to be crucified (xv. 16 ff.): "And the soldiers led him away within the court, which is the Praetorium; and they call together the whole band. And they clothe him with purple, and plaiting a crown of thorns, they put it on him; and they begin to salute him, Hail, King of the Jews! And they smote his head with a reed, and did spit upon him, and bowing their knees, worshipped him. And when they had mocked him, they took off from him the purple, and put on him his garments, and they led him out to crucify him." Of course it is unnecessary to point out how these two accounts depend upon each other. The same representation is made in the third Synoptic (xxii. 66 ff.): "And the men that held him mocked him and beat him. And they blindfolded him, and asked him, saying, Prophesy: who is he that struck thee? And many other things spake they against him, reviling him." This passes, as in the other Synoptics, in the house of the high priest, but the subsequent mocking does not take place after Pilate delivers Jesus to be crucified, but after he has been examined by Herod (xxiii. 11): "And Herod with his soldiers set him at nought, and mocked him, and arraying him in gorgeous apparel sent him back to Pilate." In the fourth Gospel there is only the one scene of mockery, and that is placed where Jesus is scourged by the order of Pilate (xix. 2): "And the soldiers plaited a crown of thorns and put it on his head, and arrayed him in a purple garment; and they came unto him, and said: Hail, King of the Jews! and they struck him with their hands." In many respects this is the most incredible of the four narratives, for the scene is reported as taking place in the presence of Pilate and before his final condemnation of Jesus; and in the very next verse (4) it is said: "And Pilate went out again, and saith unto them, Behold, I bring him out to you, that ye may know that I find no crime in him. Jesus therefore came out, wearing the crown of thorns and the purple garment. And Pilate saith unto them; Behold the man!" Although this scene, which has been the delight of artists ever since, is so picturesque, it is quite evident that it is opposed to all that we have in the Synoptics, as well as in our fragment, and that the representation of Pilate allowing his soldiers in his presence to act in such a way, not to speak of the scourging, to a man accused before him, of whom he so strongly declares, "I find no crime in him," is quite inadmissible. The narrative in Peter is at variance with all these accounts, whilst reproducing a similar tradition, and not varying more from our Gospels than they do from each other. The variation, however, is not that of a writer compiling a narrative from the canonical Gospels, but the distinct representation of one independently making use of similar, but separate, materials.

We have already discussed, in connection with Justin's reference, the passage of Peter in which it is said that "they clad him with purple and set him on a seat of judgment, saying: Judge justly, King of Israel." Of course it is argued by some that this is derived from the fourth Gospel, on the strength of the words just quoted: ἐκάθισαν αὐτὸν ἐπὶ καθέδραν κρίσεως, which are compared with the ἐκάθισεν ἐπὶ βήματος of the fourth Gospel. It is said that Archbishop Whately used to render these words "and set him on the judgment seat," understanding the verb καθίζειν to be used transitively, and thus stating that Pilate actually set Jesus in mockery upon a judgment seat. It is suggested that both Justin, as we have seen, and Peter may have misunderstood the passage, and based their statement upon it. Now, although it must be admitted that the Greek may be rendered in this way, yet it would be necessary to add αὐτὸν to justify such use of the verb. In connection with this argument they cite the words of Isaiah lviii. 2, in the Septuagint version, referred to by Justin: "For as the prophet said, they dragged him, and set him on the judgment seat, and said: Judge for us!" The Septuagint has: αἰτεῖτέ με νῦν κρίσιν δικαίαν ... λέγοντες. It is asserted that the idea of setting Jesus on the judgment seat came from the passage of the fourth Gospel which is quoted above, understood transitively. The representation that Pilate actually set Jesus on the judgment seat, if linguistically defensible, is rejected by most critics and, as has already been mentioned, amongst others by the Revisers of the New Testament. The words used for "seat of judgment" in the fragment, ἐπὶ καθέδραν κρίσεως, differ entirely from the ἐπὶ βήματος of the fourth Gospel. The analogous "Prophesy unto us, thou Christ: who is he that struck thee?" and the "Hail, King of the Jews," are, of course, widely different from the representation in Peter, in which the "Judge justly!" is evidently in mockery of the Messianic claims of Jesus, and the "King of Israel" a peculiarity of this Gospel to which we shall have to refer again further on. The statement that "others pierced him with a reed" is also a variation from the canonical Gospels, which only say, "they took the reed and smote him on the head." The fourth Gospel has alone the representation of the soldier piercing the side of Jesus with a spear "that the Scripture might be fulfilled.... They shall look on him whom they pierced," but in our fragment the representation is made casually and without any appearance of dogmatic intention. The crown of thorns is used merely incidentally, as in the case of the Synoptics, and without the artistic prominence given to it in the fourth Gospel.

There is no mention in Peter of any one bearing the cross, and in this there is a departure from the narrative both of the Synoptics and of the fourth Gospel. The Synoptics have in common, as usual, the story regarding its being laid on the shoulders of Simon of Cyrene (Matt. xxvii. 32 f., Mark xv. 21 f., Luke xxiii. 26 f.), whom they compelled to carry it to Calvary. The fourth Gospel not only omits this episode, but contradicts it in good set terms (xix. 17): "They took Jesus, therefore; and he went out, bearing the cross for himself, unto the place called 'The place of a skull.'"

Peter does not enter into any intermediate detail, but at once says: 10. "And they brought two malefactors and crucified between them the Lord; but he kept silence, as feeling no pain." The canonical Gospels all narrate the crucifixion of the two malefactors, but the various terms in which this is done must be given for comparison. Matthew says (xxvii. 38): "Then are there crucified with him two robbers, one on the right hand, and one on the left." Mark uses almost the same words (xv. 27). Luke, with some exercise of his usual constructive style, says the same thing (xxiii. 32 f.): "And there were also two others, malefactors, led with him to be put to death. And when they came unto the place which is called 'The skull,' there they crucified him and the malefactors, one on the right hand and the other on the left." The fourth Gospel reads (xix. 17 f.): "They took Jesus therefore; and he went out, bearing the cross for himself, unto the place called 'The place of a skull,' which is called in Hebrew Golgotha: where they crucified him, and with him two others, on either side one, and Jesus in the midst." The only remark necessary here is that in Peter the common tradition is given with independence and simplicity.

It is only in the last words of the verse that we have an important variation. "But he kept silence, as feeling no pain." We have already referred to this as one of the recognised Docetic passages of the fragment, although there is no necessity to read it in this sense. Mr. Murray has pointed out a passage in Origen in which that writer "gives them an innocent" (that is, not a Docetic) "interpretation."

Et in his omnibus unigenita virtus nocita non est, sicut nec passa est aliquid, facta pro nobis maledictum, cum naturaliter benedictio esset; sed cum benedictio esset, consumpsit et solvit et dissipavit omnem maledictionem humanam. Orig. in Mat. 125.86

Although there is no exact parallel to this in our Gospels, it is worth a moment's notice that the silence of Jesus during the trial is mentioned as remarkable and as exciting wonder. We have not in our fragment, unfortunately, the earlier part of the trial, and cannot, therefore, see whether the words used have any reference to previous representations. In Matt. xxvii. 12 f., it is said: "And when he was accused by the chief priests and elders, he answered nothing. Then saith Pilate unto him, Hearest thou not how many things they witness against thee? And he gave him no answer, not even to one word: insomuch that the governor marvelled greatly." An almost identical account is given in Mark. In Luke it is to the questioning of Herod that Jesus is silent (xxiii. 9): "And he [Herod] questioned him in many words; but he answered him nothing." In the fourth Gospel not only is nothing said of the silence of Jesus, but he is represented as answering freely—and in the tone of the discourses which characterise that Gospel—the questions of Pilate. Now, in the Synoptics, we have a silence described, which causes the governor to marvel greatly, that is not, however, when we go into detail, very marked in them, and is excluded by the fourth Gospel. Can a silence have been referred to, in the original tradition, which was connected with the trial, instead of the cross, because it began to receive a Docetic application, but which we have, in its earlier form, in Peter?

In our fragment, the narrative continues: 11. "And as they set up the cross they wrote thereon: 'This is the King of Israel.'" We have here a continuation of the indefinite "they," which it becomes at every step more impossible to identify otherwise than with the soldiers. It is a most curious circumstance, frequently pointed out, that no two of the Gospels agree even in so plain a matter as should be the inscription on the cross, and that the Gospel of Peter differs from them all. Matthew gives it (xxvii. 37): "This is Jesus, the King of the Jews;" Mark (xv. 26): "The King of the Jews;" Luke (xxiii. 38): "This is the King of the Jews," and John (xix. 19): "Jesus of Nazareth, the King of the Jews." The author of the fourth Gospel adds the statement that this title "was written in Hebrew, in Latin, and in Greek," and further gives a conversation between the "chief priests of the Jews" and Pilate, in which they complain of this superscription, and wish it to be put "that he said, I am King of the Jews," to which Pilate answered briefly, "What I have written, I have written." With so many forms to select from, is it reasonable to suppose that Peter would have invented another superscription, if these four Gospels had actually been before him?87

The author of the fragment continues: 12. "And they laid the clothes before him and distributed them and cast lots (λαχμὸν ἔβαλον) for them." In Matthew (xxvii. 35) it is said: "And when they had crucified him, they parted his garments among them, casting lots" (βάλλοντες κλῆρον); in Mark (xv. 24): "And they crucify him, and part his garments among them, casting lots (βάλλοντες κλῆρον) upon them, what each should take." In Luke there is a similar statement (xxiii. 34): "And parting his garments among them, they cast lots" (ἔβαλον κλῆρον). In the fourth Gospel, as usual, we have further details (xix. 23 f.): "The soldiers therefore, when they had crucified Jesus, took his garments and made four parts, to every soldier a part; and also the coat: now the coat was without seam, woven from the top throughout. They said therefore one to another, Let us not rend it, but cast lots (λάχωμεν) for it, whose it shall be: that the scripture might be fulfilled, which saith, They parted my garments among them, and upon my vesture did they cast lots" (ἔβαλον κλῆρον). In discussing the connection of Justin with the Gospel of Peter, we have already partly dealt with this passage, and now confront it with all the four Gospels. It is obvious that the language of the three Synoptics is distinct from that of Peter, who uses the unusual word λαχμός, not found in any of the Gospels. The fourth Gospel has the common verb λαγχάνω, whilst the quotation from the Psalm (xxii. 18), from which the whole episode emanates, uses the expression common to the three Synoptics, ἔβαλον κλῆρον. There is no reason for supposing that Peter makes use of our Gospels here, and in the absence of other evidence, the λαχμός is decisive proof of his independence.

The author of our fragment, after the crucifixion, has none of the mocking speeches of the four Gospels, and he ignores the episode of the penitent thief, as it is told in the third Synoptic, but he relates, instead, how one of the malefactors rebuked the mockers: 13. "But one of these malefactors reproved them, saying: We have suffered this for the evil which we wrought, but this man who has become the saviour of men, what wrong hath he done you? 14. And they were angry with him, and they commanded that his legs should not be broken, in order that he might die in torment."

It will be remembered that the episode of the penitent thief is given in Luke only, and that the other Gospels do not mention any utterance of the two malefactors said to have been crucified with Jesus. Luke's narrative reads (xxiii. 39 f.): "And one of the malefactors which were hanged railed on him, saying: Art not thou the Christ? Save thyself and us. But the other answered, and rebuking him said, Dost thou not even fear God, seeing thou art in the same condemnation? And we indeed justly: for we receive the due reward of our deeds; but this man hath done nothing amiss. And he said, Jesus, remember me when thou comest in thy kingdom. And he said unto him, Verily, I say unto thee, To-day shalt thou be with me in Paradise." That all the other Gospels should have excluded an incident like this, supposing it to have really occurred, is very extraordinary, and the only conclusion to which we can come is either that it did not occur, or that they were ignorant of it. Peter has evidently got an earlier form of the story, without those much later touches with which the third Synoptist has embellished it. The malefactor rebukes the Jews and not his fellow, and if he display a piety which is not very natural under the circumstances, he is not in this more remarkable than his counterpart in the third Synoptic. That the author was not acquainted with the form in Luke, and is quite uninfluenced by it, seems to us manifest.

This is rendered all the more apparent by the continuation in Peter, in which, instead of any reply from Jesus, or any promise of Paradise, there is connected with the rebuke of the malefactor on the cross a view of the crurifragium which is quite foreign to the canonical Gospels. When the malefactor had spoken, instead of their being mollified, the fragment declares: "And they were angry with him, and they commanded that his legs should not be broken, in order that he might die in torment." Now, here, there is a point which demands examination. To whom does this sentence refer? to Jesus or the malefactor? It is at first sight, and apart from consideration of the style of the writer, a reference to the latter, but on closer examination it seems to us more probable that the writer intended it to apply to Jesus. In any case, it is a point in which so remarkable a version of the story is concerned that it cannot but be considered as very singular that most apologetic critics have passed it over without any notice whatever, and apparently treated the order not to break the legs as applying to the malefactor and not to Jesus.88 In the first edition of his article on the fragment, Harnack took the view that more probably the malefactor was indicated here, but in his second edition he withdraws this, and adopts the conclusion that the reference of αὐτῷ to Jesus "appears more acceptable, both on account of John xix. 32 f., and also on account of the context."89 Zahn considers the whole episode in Peter as a caricature of the Gospel tradition, through the author's hatred of the Jews, and refers only indirectly to the version of the crurifragium as drawn by the caricaturist from the "Motive" of the fourth Evangelist, but does not further go into the matter than to say, with mysterious reticence: "Whoever is of another opinion should keep it to himself"!90 Hilgenfeld, who considers the whole passage as quite independent of our Gospels, regrets Harnack's change of view, and applies the αὐτῷ to the malefactor;91 but many able critics, with equal decision, understand it as a reference to Jesus,92 and Harnack himself, of course, sees that, even adopting his later view, there is a clear contradiction in the account in Peter to the representation of the fourth Gospel. To independent criticism, the result is a matter of indifference, and we shall merely state the reasons which seem to favour the view that the passage was intended to apply to Jesus, and then present the consequence if it be referred to the malefactor.

Throughout the whole of the fragment, the sustained purpose of the author is to present Jesus in the strongest light, and subordinate everything to the representation of his sufferings and resurrection. At the part we are considering, the narrative is of the closest and most condensed character: the crucifixion between the two malefactors; the silence as feeling no pain; the superscription on the cross, and the parting of the garments, are all told without wasting a word. The reproach of the malefactor, apparently addressed to those who are parting the garments, is more intended to increase our sympathy for Jesus than to excite it for the speaker, and it is certainly not the writer's purpose to divert our attention from the sufferings of Jesus by presenting those of the generous malefactor. Rather it is to show that the more the high character and mission of Jesus are set forth, the more bitter becomes the animosity and hatred of the Jews; so that, to the remonstrance of the malefactor, they reply by increasing the sufferings of Jesus. In short, the sense of the passage seems to be "And they, being angered at what was said, commanded that the legs of Jesus should not be broken, that he might die in torment." However, let us take the view that the command was given that the malefactor's legs should not be broken, that he might die in torment. It clearly follows that, if he was to be made to suffer more by not having his legs broken, the legs of the other two must on the contrary have been broken. The command not to break his legs necessarily implies that otherwise the legs of all would have been so broken. There is really no escape from this inference. Now the crurifragium is here represented as an act of mercy and to hasten death, but in the immediate context we are told that they were troubled and anxious lest the sun should have set whilst Jesus still lived. No anxiety of this kind is felt lest the malefactors should still be alive, and why? Because if an exception to breaking the legs had been made in one case, and that exception had been Jesus, the malefactors would be supposed to be already dead. If, on the contrary, the legs of Jesus had been broken, they would not have feared his being alive, but rather the malefactor whose legs had not been broken. Jesus having been left to linger in torment is still alive, and the potion of vinegar and gall is given to him to produce death, and not to the malefactor. The whole context, therefore, shows that no means such as the crurifragium had been used with Jesus to hasten death, and that the potion was at last given for the purpose. If, on the other hand, the legs of Jesus were actually broken, and not those of the malefactor, a most complete contradiction of the account in the fourth Gospel is given, and of the Scripture which is said in it to have been fulfilled.

Let us now see how the account in Peter compares with that in the fourth Gospel, on the hypothesis that the writer intended to represent that, in order to lengthen his sufferings, the legs of Jesus were not broken. It would follow that the crurifragium was applied to the two malefactors, and that Jesus was left to a lingering death by the cruel animosity of his executioners. It will, of course, be remembered that the fourth Gospel is the only one which recounts the crurifragium. In this narrative it is not represented as an act of mercy to shorten the sufferings of the crucified. It is said (xix. 31 f.): "The Jews therefore, because it was the Preparation, that the bodies should not remain on the cross upon the Sabbath (for the day of that Sabbath was a high day), asked of Pilate that their legs might be broken, and that they might be taken away. The soldiers therefore came, and brake the legs of the first, and of the other which was crucified with him; but when they came to Jesus, and saw that he was dead already, they brake not his legs ... that the Scripture might be fulfilled, A bone of him shall not be broken." The object of the author in relating this is obviously dogmatic, and to show the fulfilment of Scripture, but the way in which he brings the matter about is awkward, to say the least of it, and not so natural as that adopted by Peter. The soldiers brake the legs "of the first,"—and by this description they imply that they begin at one end—and proceed to the second, who would be Jesus; but not so, for having broken the legs "of the first, and of the other," they come to Jesus, whom they must have passed over. Is this passing over of Jesus in the first instance a slight indication of a tradition similar to that which has been reproduced in Peter? However this may be, it is quite clear that, while the fourth Gospel deals with the episode purely from a dogmatic point of view, this is completely absent from Peter, who even leaves it in doubt, and as a problem for critics, whether the legs of Jesus were broken or not, and evidently does not give a thought to the Johannine representation of Jesus as the Paschal lamb. Whichever way the passage in Peter is construed, the entire independence of the writer from the influence of the fourth Gospel seems to be certain.

The fragment proceeds:

15. Now it was mid-day, and a darkness covered all Judaea, and they were troubled and anxious lest the sun should have set whilst he still lived, for it is written for them: "The sun must not go down upon one put to death." 16. And one of them said: "Give him to drink gall with vinegar;" and having mixed, they gave him to drink. 17. And they fulfilled all things, and completed their sins upon their own head. 18. Now many went about with lights, thinking that it was night, and some fell.93 The three Synoptics have an account of this darkness in words which nearly repeat each other. Matthew xxvii. 45: "Now from the sixth hour there was darkness over all the earth (ἐπὶ πᾶσαν τὴν γῆν) until the ninth hour." Mark (xv. 33): "And when the sixth hour was come, there was darkness over the whole earth (ἐφ' ὅλην τὴν γῆν) until the ninth hour." In Luke (xxiii. 44 f.) other details are, as usual, added: "And it was now about the sixth hour, and a darkness came over the whole earth (ἐφ' ὅλην τὴν γῆν) until the ninth hour, the sun failing [or rather 'being eclipsed,' τοῦ ἡλίου ἐκλειπόντος]."94 It is a very extraordinary circumstance that, whether a miraculous eclipse or not, whether this darkness came over the whole land or the whole earth, the fourth Gospel has either not believed in it, or thought it unworthy of mention, for no reference to the astonishing phenomenon is found in it. Peter, in a manner quite different from the Synoptics, and in fuller detail, describes this darkness and its effect upon the people. For the second time, he refers to a portion of the Jewish law, interpreted from Deut. xxi. 23, to illustrate the anxiety which the supposed going down of the sun had excited. This expression does not favour any theory of his being acquainted with the third Synoptic.

The most important part of the passage is that in v. 16: "And one of them said: 'Give him to drink gall with vinegar;' and having mixed they gave him to drink." This proceeding is represented as the result of their anxiety at the sun going down whilst Jesus still lived, and the gall and vinegar are regarded as a potion to hasten death. This view is foreign to all of our Gospels. In Matthew xxvii. 48, when Jesus gives the loud cry, "My God, my God," &c., we read: "And straightway one of them ran and took a sponge and filled it with vinegar, and put it on a reed, and gave him to drink. And the rest said, Let be; let us see whether Elijah cometh to save him." In Mark (xv. 36) the representation is almost the same. In both of these cases death follows almost immediately. In Luke (xxiii. 36) a very different representation is made. There is no such cry connected with it, but it is simply said: "And the soldiers also mocked him, coming to him, offering him vinegar, and saying, If thou art the King of the Jews, save thyself." In John the episode has quite another, and purely dogmatic, tendency (xix. 28 ff.). It commences immediately after the episode of the mother and the beloved disciple, and without any previous cry: "After this Jesus, knowing that all things are now finished, that the Scripture might be accomplished, saith, I thirst. There was set there a vessel full of vinegar; so they put a sponge full of vinegar upon hyssop, and brought it to his mouth. When Jesus therefore had received the vinegar, he said, It is finished; and he bowed his head and gave up his spirit." Of course the Scripture which is represented as being thus fulfilled is Psalm lxix. 21: "... and in my thirst they gave me vinegar to drink." In all of these Gospels, the potion is simply vinegar, and being evidently associated with this Psalm, it is in no way connected with any baleful intention. The Psalm, however, commences: "They gave me also gall for my meat," and in connection with the combination of gall with vinegar in Peter, as a potion to hasten death, it may be mentioned that the word which is in the Psalm translated "gall" may equally well be rendered "poison"—as, indeed, is also the case with the Latin "fel." Peter, by what is said in v. 17—"And they fulfilled all things, and completed their sins upon their own head"—is more anxious to show that the Jews had put the final touch to their cruel work, in thus completing the death of Jesus, than to refer to the mere fulfilment of the Psalm. The only Gospel which mentions gall is the first Synoptic, in which it is said (xxvii. 34) that when they had brought Jesus to Golgotha before the crucifixion, "They gave him wine to drink mingled with gall; and when he had tasted it, he would not drink." This is a very different representation from that of Peter, and the potion was obviously that often offered to persons about to suffer, in order to dull sensation. The passage might almost be represented as Docetic, from the writer's intention to show that Jesus refused to adopt a usual method of diminishing pain. There does not seem to be any warrant for supposing that the author of the fragment derived the passage we are examining from our Gospels, from which it is in all essential points distinct.

The narrative of the fragment continues, v. 19: "And the Lord cried aloud, saying, 'Power, my Power, thou hast forsaken me!' (ἡ δύναμίς μου, ἡ δύναμις, κατέλειψάς με), and having spoken, he was taken up (ἀνελήφθη)." In this passage there is a very marked departure from the tradition followed by our four Gospels. Before considering the actual words of the cry recorded here, it may be desirable to form a general idea of the representations of the Synoptists and of the author of the fourth Gospel regarding the words spoken from the cross.

It might naturally have been supposed that, in describing the course of so solemn an event as the crucifixion, unusual care, securing unusual agreement, would have been exercised by Christian writers, and that the main facts—and still more the last words—of the great Master would have been collected. As we have already seen, however, in no portion of the history is there greater discrepancy in the accounts in the four Gospels, nor greater contradictions upon every point.

The same is the case with regard to what has still to be examined, and notably in the words and cries from the cross. In the first two Synoptics, with the exception of the inarticulate cry "with a loud voice" (Matt. xxvii. 50, Mark xv. 37) when yielding up his spirit, the only utterance recorded is one resembling that in Peter (Matt. xxvii. 46, Mark xv. 34): "Eloi, Eloi, lama sabachthani? that is, My God, my God, why hast thou forsaken me?"95 (ἠλωί ἠλωί λαμὰ σαβαχθανεί; τοῦτ' ἔστιν; Θεέ μου, Θεέ μου, ἵνα τί με ἐγκατέλιπες?). It will be observed that here there is a demonstration of great accuracy, in actually giving the original words used and translating them, which is uncommon in the Gospels. It is all the more extraordinary that neither of the other Gospels gives this cry at all, but that they represent Jesus as uttering quite different words. The third Synoptist represents Jesus immediately after the crucifixion as saying (Luke xxiii. 34): "Father, forgive them; for they know not what they do." The other evangelists do not evince any knowledge of this, and as little of the episode of the penitent thief (xxiii. 39 ff.)—which we have already considered—in which Jesus uses the remarkable words (v. 43): "Verily I say unto thee, To-day shalt thou be with me in Paradise." In Luke, further, the inarticulate cry is interpreted (xxiii. 46): "And when Jesus had cried with a loud voice, he said, Father, into thy hands I commend my spirit; and having said this, he gave up the ghost." Of this the other Synoptists do not say anything. The author of the fourth Gospel has quite a different account to give from any of the Synoptics. He seems to be ignorant of the words which they report, and substitutes others of which they seem to know nothing. The episode of the penitent thief is replaced by the scene between Jesus and his mother and the disciple "whom he loved" (xix. 25 ff.). Not only is this touching episode apparently unknown to the Synoptists, but the proximity of the women to the cross is in direct contradiction to what we find in Matthew and Mark, for in the former (xxvii. 55 f.) it is said that many women, "among whom was Mary Magdalene, and Mary the mother of James and Joses, and the mother of the sons of Zebedee" were "beholding afar off;" and the latter (xv. 40 f.) reports: "And there were also women beholding from afar: among whom were both Mary Magdalene and Mary the mother of James the less and of Joses, and Salome." In the fourth Gospel (xix. 28), Jesus is moreover reported to have said "I thirst," in order "that the Scripture might be accomplished"—a fact which is not recorded in any of the Synoptics—and having received vinegar upon hyssop, "he said, It is finished, and he bowed his head and gave up his spirit." The last words of Jesus, therefore, according to the fourth Gospel, are different from any found in the three Synoptics. The Gospel of Peter differs as completely from the four canonical Gospels as they do from each other, and the whole account of the agony on the cross given in it is quite independent of them.

The only words recorded by Peter as uttered on the cross are those quoted higher up: "Power, my Power, thou hast forsaken me," the second "my" being omitted, and the question of the two Synoptics, "Why hast thou forsaken me?" being changed into a declaration by the omission of ἵνα τί (or εἰς τί, Mark). We have already discussed the Docetic nature of this cry, and are now only considering it in relation to our Gospels. It is obvious that the substitution of "Power, my Power" for "My God, my God" introduces quite a different order of ideas, especially followed as it is by the remarkable statement: "He was taken up." Eusebius tells us that Aquila rendered the words of Psalm xxii. 1— whence the first two Synoptists take their cry—as ἰσχυρέ μου, ἰσχυρέ μου ("My strong one, my strong one"), but that the more exact sense was ἰσχύσ μου, ἰσχύς μου ("My strength, my strength");96 but though this is interesting as in some degree connecting the cry with the Psalm, it does not lessen the discrepancy between Peter and the Gospels, or in the least degree favour the theory of acquaintance with them.

The expression used to describe what follows this cry completes the wide separation between them: "And having spoken, he was taken up" (ἀνελήφθη). In the first Synoptic, after his cry (xxvii. 50), "he yielded up the spirit" (ἀφῆκεν τὸ πνεῦμα), whilst the second and third say (Mark xv. 37, Luke xxiii. 46), "he gave up the ghost" ἐξέπνευσεν, and the fourth Gospel reads (xix. 30), "he delivered up the spirit" (παρέδωκεν τὸ πνεῦμα). The representation in Peter is understood to be that the divine descended upon the human Christ in the form of the dove at baptism, and immediately ascended to Heaven again at his death. There is not here, however, any declaration of a double Christ, or any denial of the reality of the Christ's body, such as characterised the later Docetae; indeed, the fact that the dead body is still always spoken of as that of "the Lord" seems distinctly to exclude this, as does the whole subsequent narrative. Whatever Docetism there may be in this fragment is of the earliest type, if indeed its doctrines can be clearly traced at all; but undoubtedly when the sect had become pronounced heretics, orthodox Christians detected their subtle influence in much that was in itself very simple and harmless.

The fragment continues (v. 20): "And the same hour the veil of the Temple of Jerusalem was torn in twain" (διεράγη τὸ καταπέτασμα τοῦ ναοῦ τῆς Ἰερουσαλὴμ εἰς δύο). This expression the "temple of Jerusalem" is one of those which seem to indicate that the Gospel was written away from Palestine, but in this it probably differs little from most of the canonical Gospels. The statement regarding the veil of the temple is almost the same in the first two Synoptics (Matt. xxvii. 51, Mark xv. 38). "And behold, the veil of the temple was rent in twain from the top to the bottom" (τὸ καταπέτασμα τοῦ ναοῦ ἐσχίσθη ἀπ' ἄνωθεν ἕως κάτω εἰς δύο). In Luke (xxiii. 45) the rent is "in the midst" (μέσον), but otherwise the words are the same. The use of διεράγη instead of the ἐσχίσθη of the three Synoptics is characteristic. The fourth Gospel, strange to say, does not record at all this extraordinary phenomenon of the rending in twain of the veil of the temple. There are some further peculiarities which must be pointed out. The third Synoptist sets the rending of the veil before Jesus cried with a loud voice and gave up the ghost; whilst in Matthew and Mark it is after the cry and giving up the spirit. Moreover, in Matthew, it is associated with an earthquake, and the rending of the rocks and opening of tombs, and the astounding circumstance that many bodies of the saints that had fallen asleep were raised, and coming forth out of the tombs after his resurrection they entered into the holy city, and appeared unto many: of all of which the other three Gospels make no mention, nor does Peter in this connection.

The narrative in the fragment continues:

21. And then they took out the nails from the hands of the Lord, and laid him upon the earth; and the whole earth quaked, and great fear came [upon them]. 22. Then the sun shone out, and it was found to be the ninth hour. 23. Now the Jews were glad and gave his body to Joseph, that he might bury it, for he had beheld the good works that he did.97 24. And he took the Lord and washed him, and wrapped him in linen, and brought him into his own grave, called "Joseph's Garden."
This passage is full of independent peculiarities. Although none of the canonical Gospels, except Matthew, says anything of an earthquake, and the first Synoptist associates it with the moment when Jesus "gave up the ghost," Peter narrates that when the body of the Lord was unloosed from the cross, the moment it was laid on the ground the whole earth quaked beneath the awful burden: a representation almost grander than anything in the four Gospels.

The canonical Gospels do not speak of the nails being taken out, and although Peter states that they were removed from the hands, he does not refer to the feet. The fourth is the only canonical Gospel that speaks of the nails at all, and there it is not in connection with the crucifixion, but the subsequent appearance to the disciples and the incredulity of Thomas (xx. 20, 25, 27). Here also, only the marks in the hands are referred to. The difference of the two representations is so great that there can really be no question of dependence, and those who are so eager to claim the use of the fourth Gospel simply because it is the only one that speaks of "nails" ("the print of the nails") might perhaps consider that the idea of crucifixion and the cross might well be independently associated with a reference to the nails by which the victim was generally attached. In the third Synoptic (xxiv. 39), the inference is inevitable that both hands and feet were supposed to be nailed. When the report, "The Lord is risen," is brought to the eleven, Jesus is represented as standing in their midst and assuring them that he was not a spirit, by saying: "See my hands and my feet, that it is I myself"—meaning of course the prints of the nails in both. The statement in Peter that on the occurrence of the earthquake "great fear came [upon them]" (φόβος μέγας ἐγένετο) is not even mentioned in Matthew when he narrates the earthquake, which he represents as occurring when Jesus expired. The expression is characteristic of the author, who uses it elsewhere.

The representation that the sun shone out and that the Jews were glad when they found it was the ninth hour, and that consequently their law, twice quoted by the author, would not be broken, is limited to the fragment; as is also the statement that they gave his body to Joseph that he might bury it, "for he had beheld the good works that he did." As we have already seen, the canonical Gospels represent Joseph as going to Pilate at this time and begging for the body of Jesus, and it will be remembered that, in Mark (xv. 44), it is said that "Pilate marvelled if he were already dead," and called the centurion to ascertain the fact before he granted the body. In Peter, the body was of course given in consequence of the previous order, when Pilate asked Herod for it.

Joseph is represented, here, as only washing the body and wrapping it in linen (λαβὼν δὲ τὸν κύριον ἔλουσε καὶ εἴλησε σινδόνι). The first Synoptist (xxvii. 59) says that Joseph took the body and "wrapped it in a clean linen cloth" (ἐνετύλιξεν αὐτὸ [ἐν] σινδόνι καθαρᾷ). Mark similarly describes that (xv. 46), bringing "a linen cloth and taking him down, he wound him in the linen cloth" (καθελὼν αὐτὸν ἐνείλησεν τῇ σινδόνι). The third Synoptist has nearly the same statement and words. The fourth Gospel has a much more elaborate account to give (xix. 38 ff.). Joseph goes to Pilate asking that he may take away the body, and Pilate gives him leave. He comes and takes away the body. "And there came also Nicodemus ... bringing a mixture of myrrh and aloes, about a hundred pound weight. So they took the body of Jesus and bound it in linen clothes (καὶ ἔδησαν αὐτὸ ὀθονίοις) with the spices, as the custom of the Jews is to bury." This account is quite different from that in the Synoptics, and equally so from Peter's, which approximates much more nearly to that in the latter.

Peter says that Joseph then "brought him into his own grave, called 'Joseph's Garden' " (εἰσήγαγεν εἰς ἴδιον τάφον καλούμενον Κῆπον Ἰωσήφ). The account of the tomb is much more minute in the canonical Gospels. In Matthew (xxvii. 60), Joseph is said to lay the body "in his own new tomb (μνημείῳ), which he had hewn out in the rock; and he rolled a great stone to the door of the tomb (μνημείου) and departed." In Mark (xv. 46), he lays him "in a tomb (μνήματι) which had been hewn out of a rock; and he rolled a stone against the door of the tomb" (μνημείου). Luke has a new detail to chronicle (xxiii. 53): Joseph lays him "in a tomb (μνηματί) that was hewn in stone, where never man had yet lain." The first two Synopists, it will be observed, say that Joseph rolls a stone against the entrance to the tomb: but neither Luke nor Peter has this detail, though the former leaves it to be inferred that it had been done, for (xxiv. 2) the women who came on the first day of the week find the stone rolled away from the tomb. In Peter, on the contrary, the stone is rolled against the tomb by the guard and others later, as we shall presently see.

In the fourth Gospel, the account has further and different details, agreeing, however, with the peculiar statement of Luke (xix. 41 f.): "Now in the place where he was crucified there was a garden (κῆπος), and in the garden a new tomb (μνημεῖον) wherein was never man yet laid. There then, because of the Jews' Preparation (for the tomb [μνημεῖον] was nigh at hand), they laid Jesus." Some stress has been laid upon the point that both Peter and the fourth Gospel use the word "garden," and that none of the Synoptics have it, and as these critics seem to go upon the principle that any statement in Peter which happens to be in any canonical Gospel, even although widely different in treatment, must have been derived from that Gospel, and not from any similar written or traditional source, from which that Gospel derived it, they argue that this shows dependence on the fourth Gospel. There is certainly no evidence of dependence here. In Peter, the grave (τάφος) is simply said to be called "Joseph's Garden" (Κῆπον Ἰωσηφ),98 and described as "his own grave." The fourth Gospel does not identify the garden as Joseph's at all, but says that "in the place where he was crucified there was a garden," and in it "a tomb" (μνημεῖον), and the reason given for taking the body thither is not that it belonged to Joseph, but that the tomb "was nigh at hand," and that on account of the Jews' Preparation they laid it there. The whole explanation seems to exclude the idea that the writer knew that it belonged to Joseph. Peter simply contributes a new detail to the common tradition. There is no appearance of his deriving this from our canonical Gospels, from which he differs in substance and in language. Neither Peter nor the Synoptics know anything of the co-operation of Nicodemus.

The narrative in the fragment continues:

25. Then the Jews and the elders and the priests, seeing the evil they had done to themselves, began to beat their breasts (ἤρξαντο κόπτεσθαι) and to say: "Woe for our sins; judgment draweth nigh and the end of Jerusalem."
We have already discussed this passage in connection with the "Diatessaron," and have now only to consider it as compared with our Gospels. There is no equivalent in any of them, except that the third Synoptist (xxiii. 48) says that when Jesus gave up the ghost: "All the multitude that came together to this sight, when they beheld the things that were done, returned smiting their breasts (τύπτοντες τὰ στήθη ὑπέστρεφον)." The reason for this change of mood is, of course, the eclipse and consequent darkness in the third Synoptic, and the earthquake and darkness in Peter; but in the former "all the multitude" smite their breasts, and in the latter "the Jews and the elders and the priests." It may be suggested whether the words inserted in the ancient Latin Codex of St. Germain, "Vae nobis, quae facta sunt hodie propter peccata nostra, appropinquavit enim desolatio Hierusalem,"99 may not have been taken from our Gospel of Peter, for an expansion of the original text of the third Synoptic, by the author of this version.

The common reference of the fragment is to "the Jews," "the Jews and the elders and the priests," "the scribes and Pharisees and elders," and "the elders and scribes." Throughout the same part of the narrative in Matthew, we have "the scribes and elders," "chief priests and elders of the people" (this, most frequently), "chief priests with the scribes and elders," and in speaking of the guard at the sepulchre, "the chief priests and the

Pharisees." In Mark, the same leaders are named, whilst in Luke we have "the chief priests and captains of the Temple and elders," "the elders of the people and both the chief priests and scribes," and, repeatedly, the "chief priests and rulers." The fourth Gospel usually cites "the chief priests and Pharisees," "chief captains and officers of the Jews," "the Jews," and "the chief priests of the Jews." There is more analogy, in this respect, between the fragment and the fourth Gospel than between it and the Synoptics.

We come now to an important and characteristic part of the fragment:

26. And I, with my companions, was mourning, and being pierced in spirit we hid ourselves; for we were sought for by them as malefactors, and as desiring to burn the temple. 27. Over all these things, however, we were fasting, and sat mourning and weeping night and day until the Sabbath.
There is no parallel to this passage in our Gospels, but in the statement that the Apostles had hidden themselves (and—taken in connection with v. 59, where the same fact is again mentioned—this means all the twelve) we have here agreement with the narrative of the first and second Synoptics (Matt. xxvi. 56; Mark xix. 50), that on the arrest of Jesus "all the disciples left him and fled." This passage seems to exclude the incident of the sword and Malchus which, as Hilgenfeld points out,[100] is also excluded by a passage in Justin; the denial of Peter, which Justin equally passes over unmentioned; and the episode of the "beloved disciple" by the cross. The reason given for hiding themselves, that they were accused of wishing to burn the temple, has some connection with the tradition, that testimony had been given against Jesus that he had said he could destroy this temple and build it in three days (Matt. xxvi. 60; Mark xiv. 58).[101] The passage is one of those in which the writer speaks in the first person and represents himself as an Apostle, which

he still more clearly does, v. 60, where he distinctly calls himself Simon Peter.

The account that the Apostles were fasting and sat mourning and weeping "night and day until the Sabbath" (νυκτὸς καὶ ἡμέρας ἕως τοῦ σαββάτου) opens out an interesting problem. As a rule, the Greek expression would be ἡμέρας καὶ νυκτός, so if we are to take the words actually used as deliberately intended to represent the time, we should have to count at least one night and one day between the death of Jesus and the Sabbath, or in other words, that the crucifixion took place, not on Friday, but upon Thursday, which, according to the statement in v. 5, would really be the 13th Nisan. A great deal might be said in support of this view,102 but it need not be entered into here. It is probable that, as Harnack suggests,103 the author really thinks of the whole time from the Thursday night, when the arrest was made.

With the next portion of the fragment the narrative of the resurrection may be said to begin:

28. But the scribes and Pharisees and elders assembled themselves together (συναχθέντες πρὸς ἀλλήλους), hearing that all the people murmured and beat their breasts, saying, "If at his death these great signs have happened, behold how just a one he is." 29. The elders were afraid (ἐφοβήθησαν) and came to Pilate (ἦλθον πρὸς Πειλᾶτον) beseeching him and saying, 30. "Give us soldiers that we may watch his grave for three days (ἵνα φυλάξωμεν τὸ μνῆμα αὐτοῦ ἐπὶ τρεῖς ἡμέρας), lest his disciples come and steal him, and the people believe that he rose from the dead and do us evil" (μήποτε ἐλθόντες οἱ μαθηταὶ αὐτοῦ κλέψωσιν αὐτὸν καὶ ὑπολάβῃ ὁ λαὸς ὅτι ἐκ νεκρῶν ἀνέστη, καὶ ποιήσωσιν ἡμῖν κακά). 31. Pilate, therefore, gave them Petronius the centurion with soldiers to watch the tomb (μετὰ στρατιωτῶν φυλάσσειν τὸν τάφον), and with them came

the elders and scribes to the grave (τὸ μνῆμα). 32. And they rolled a great stone (κυλίσαντες λίθον μέγαν) against the centurion and the soldiers, and set it, all who were there together, at the door of the grave (μνήματος). 33. And they put seven seals (καὶ ἐπέχρισαν ἑπτὰ σφραγῖδας), and setting up a tent there they kept guard (ἐφύλαξαν). 34. And in the morning, at the dawn of the Sabbath, came a multitude from Jerusalem and the neighbourhood in order that they might see the sealed-up grave (τὸ μνημεῖον ἐσφραγισμένον).

There is no parallel to this narrative in any of our canonical Gospels except the first Synoptic, which alone mentions the circumstance that a watch was set over the sepulchre, a fact of which the other Gospels seem quite ignorant, and states that application was made to Pilate for a guard for that purpose. The account in Matthew is as follows (xxvii. 62 f.):

Now on the morrow, which is the day after the Preparation, the chief priests and the Pharisees were gathered together (συνήχθησαν) unto Pilate, saying, Sir, we remember that that deceiver said, while he was yet alive, After three days I rise again. Command therefore that the sepulchre be made sure until the third day, lest haply his disciples come and steal him away, and say unto the people, He rose from the dead: and the last error will be worse than the first (ἀσφαλισθῆναι τὸν τάφον ἕως τῆς τρίτης ἡμέρας; μήποτε ἐλθόντες οἱ μαθηταὶ κλέψωσιν αὐτόν, καὶ εἴπωσιν τῷ λαῷ, Ἡγέρθη ἀπὸ τῶν νεκρῶν; καὶ ἔσται ἡ ἐσχάτη πλάνη χείρων τῆς πρώτης). Pilate said unto them, Ye have a guard: go your way, make it as sure as ye can. So they went, and made the sepulchre sure (ἠσφαλίσαντο τὸν τάφον), sealing the stone (σφραγίσαντες τὸν λίθον), the guard being with them (μετὰ τῆς κουστωδίας).

The fact that only one of the four canonical Gospels has any reference to this episode, or betrays the slightest knowledge of any precautions taken to guard the tomb, is remarkable. The analogies in the narrative in Peter with the general account, and the similarity of the language in certain parts, together with the wide variation in details and language generally, point to the conclusion that both writers derive the episode from a similar source, but independently of each other. The casual agreement with continuous dissimilarity of statement and style, are evidence of the separate treatment of a common tradition, and put the fragment upon a very different footing from the Synoptics in relation to each other. The absence of verisimilitude is pretty nearly equal in both Gospels, but these traditions grew up, and were unconsciously rounded by the contributions of pious imagination.

In the fragment it is "the scribes and Pharisees and elders" (οἱ γραμματεῖς καὶ Φαρισαῖοι καὶ πρεσβύτεροι) who meet together, but only the "elders" go to Pilate; in the Synoptic, "the chief Priests and the Pharisees" (οἱ ἀρχιερεῖς καὶ οἱ Φαρισαῖοι) meet and go to Pilate. Pilate gives them "Petronius the centurion with soldiers" to watch the tomb; in Matthew, he gives them "a guard," bidding them make it sure; so they go and seal the stone, the guard being with them. In Peter, the "elders and scribes" go to the grave, and themselves with the soldiers, "all who were there together," roll a great stone and set it at the door of the grave. Doubtless this trait is intended to convey an impression of the great size of the stone. A curious peculiarity occurs in the statement, "they roll the stone against the centurion and the soldiers," the intention of the words probably being that, in their suspicious mood, they thus protected themselves from possible fraud on the part even of the soldiers.104 The motive for the application to Pilate, in the fragment, is fear on the part of the elders, in consequence of the murmuring and lamentation of the people, who are represented as being convinced by the great signs occurring at the death of Jesus "how just a one" he was. This is quite a variation from the Synoptic version, but both agree in the explanation given to Pilate of anxiety lest the disciples should steal the body, and say that Jesus had risen from the dead. In Matthew, they simply "seal the stone," but in the fragment they put or smear (ἐπέχρισαν) "seven seals" upon it. Some important peculiarities then occur in the narrative of Peter. They set up a tent beside the tomb and keep guard, and in the morning a multitude from Jerusalem and the neighbourhood come out to see the sealed-up grave. There is nothing corresponding to this in the Synoptic Gospel.

The narrative proceeds:

35. Now, in the night before the dawn of the Lord's day (ἡ κυριακή), whilst the soldiers were keeping guard over the place, two and two in a watch, there was a great voice in the heaven. 36. And they saw the heavens opened and two men come down from thence with great light and approach the tomb. 37. But the stone which had been laid at the door rolled of itself away by the side, and the tomb was opened and both the young men entered.

Here commences an account of the resurrection very different in every respect from that in our canonical Gospels, and the treatment of a tradition in some points necessarily common to all is evidently independent. In Matthew, the scene commences with an earthquake—earthquakes are, indeed, peculiar to the first Synoptist—(xxviii. 2 f.): "And behold there was a great earthquake; for an angel of the Lord descended from heaven, and came and rolled away the stone and sat upon it. His appearance was as lightning, and his raiment white as snow; and for fear of him the watchers did quake and become as dead men." Here only one angel comes down, whilst in Peter there are two men, whom some critics—amongst whom may be mentioned Nestle, with whom Harnack is inclined to agree, more especially as they are never called angels, but merely "two men"—identify as Moses and Elias. The angel rolls away the stone, which in Peter rolls away of itself, and sits upon it, whilst in Peter the two men enter into the tomb. No account is given in Mark of the opening of the tomb, the women simply finding the stone rolled away, and a young man (νεανίσκον) sitting on the right side arrayed in a white robe (xvi. 4 f.); the author does not mention any earthquake. In the third Synoptic (xxiv. 2 f.), the women also find the stone already rolled away from the tomb; there is no earthquake. When the women enter the tomb they do not find "the body of the Lord Jesus," but while they are perplexed two men stand by them in dazzling apparel. In the fourth Gospel (xx. 12 f.), Mary, coming to the sepulchre, sees two angels in white sitting—the one at the head, the other at the foot—where the body of Jesus had lain. Thus, to sum up, in Matthew there is one angel, in Mark one young man, in Luke two men, in the fourth Gospel two angels, and in Peter two men descend from heaven to the tomb.

Peter goes on:

38. Then these soldiers, seeing this, awakened the centurion and the elders, for they also were keeping watch. 39. And whilst they were narrating to them what they had seen, they beheld again three men coming out of the tomb and the two were supporting the one, and a cross following them. 40. And the heads of the two indeed reached up to the heaven, but that of him that was led by their hands rose above the heavens. 41. And they heard a voice from the heavens saying, "Hast thou preached to them that are sleeping?" 42. And an answer was heard from the cross: "Yea."

Of course there is nothing corresponding to this in the canonical Gospels. In Matthew, the watchers quake and become as dead men, but no such alarm is here described. The elders and soldiers see the two men who had entered the tomb come out leading a third, and the stately appearance of the three is described with Oriental extravagance.[105] Following the three is a cross, a very singular representation, more especially as the cross presently speaks. Harnack says that Duhms, who supposes a Hebraic original, conjectures that the Hebrew word, which could as well stand for "crucified" as "cross," was misunderstood by the translator, and he adds that, if the original was Aramaic, the matter becomes still simpler. However, Harnack does not seem disposed to adopt the suggestion.106 It is well known that in very early works the cross was identified with the crucified, and treated both as a type and as having a certain personality—the living and eloquent symbol of victory over death.107

The words of the voice from the heavens are: " 'Hast thou preached to them that are sleeping?' and an answer was heard from the cross: 'Yea' " (Ἐκήρυξας τοῖς κοιμωμένοις; καὶ ὑπακοὴ ἠκούετο ἀπὸ τοῦ σταυροῦ ὅτι Ναί). This is generally understood as a reference to the "descent into hell," which was early accepted as a dogma by the Church and has a place in the Creed, although its only clear mention in the New Testament occurs in 1 Peter iii. 18 f.: "Because Christ ... being put to death in the flesh, but quickened in the spirit, in which also he went and preached (ἐκήρυξεν) unto the spirits in prison, which aforetime were disobedient;" and (iv. 6): "For unto this end was the Gospel spoken unto the dead." It is a curious fact that the "Gospel according to Peter," the fragment of which is first discovered in a little volume along with a fragment of the "Apocalypse of Peter," should thus contain a reference to a doctrine, the only allusion to which in any of the canonical writings is contained in a so-called "Epistle of Peter." Hilgenfeld wishes to read κοινωμένοις instead of κοιμωμένοις, and disputes the rendering of ὑπακοή as "answer," although he admits that there is some support to this as a liturgical response.108 He would render this passage: "Du verkündigtest den Profanirten und einem Gehorsam.109 Von dem Kreuze her erschallt: Ja." He argues that there can be no question here of a descent into hell by one coming out of the grave who cannot even hold himself upright, but must be led; that, however much the inanimate body of Jesus may still be called "the Lord," his "Self" is already in death ascended to heaven; the selfless (selbstlose) body cannot possibly in the meantime have gone into Hades.110 In this conclusion, however, he is at variance with almost all critics, who generally take the view rendered above.111

The passage which we have quoted from Matthew (xxvii. 52 f.) must be recalled, in which the first Synoptic alone of the four canonical Gospels has an account of astonishing events said to have occurred at the death of Jesus: an earthquake which rent the rocks and opened the tombs, "and many bodies of the saints that were sleeping (κεκοιμημένων) were raised; and coming forth out of the tombs after his resurrection, they entered into the holy city and appeared unto many." This resurrection of the saints "that were sleeping" is associated by Eusebius with the descent into hell,112 and it is not improbable that the first Synoptist had it in his mind. It is not necessary to point out many early references to the descent into hell,113 but an interesting passage may be quoted from Justin. He accuses the Jews of omitting from the prophecy of Jeremiah in their copies of the Septuagint the following verse: "The Lord God, the Holy one of Israel, remembered his dead who lay sleeping (κεκοιμημένων) in the earth, and descended to them to bring to them the good news of his salvation."114 It is not known that the passage ever really existed in Jeremiah but, notwithstanding, Irenaeus quotes it no less than five times.115

The writer does not explain the representation of the three who came out of the tomb, two of whom were "supporting," or, as is subsequently said, leading him, or conducting him, but this figure, more stately than the others, of course, is intended to be recognised as Jesus. Too much has been said as to the weakness supposed to be here described, and Zahn, who as much as possible ridicules the whole contents of the fragment, says that "the raised Lazarus, in comparison with him, is a hero in strength and life." But is the intention here to depict weakness? No word is used which really demands that interpretation. As Dr. Swete rightly points out, "the support appears to be regarded as nominal only, since He is also said to be 'conducted' (χειραγωγούμενον)" (p. 18). It is true that χειραγωγεῖν is twice used in Acts (ix. 8, xxii. 11) to express Paul's helplessness when led by the hand after his vision on the way to Damascus, but it does not in itself imply weakness, and no other hint of feebleness is given in the fragment. The "touch me not" of the fourth Gospel, when Mary Magdalene stretches out her hand to Jesus, is quite as much a mark of weakness as this. It may not unfairly, on the other hand, be interpreted as a mark of honour, and nothing in Peter forbids this reading. If weakness were indicated, it might be taken as a Docetic representation of the condition of the human body, deprived of the divine Christ, who had ascended from the cross.

The continuation of the narrative in Peter is as different from that of our canonical Gospels as its commencement:

43. These, therefore, took counsel together whether they should go and declare these things to Pilate. 44. And whilst they were still considering, the heavens again appeared opened, and a certain man descending and going into the grave. 45. Seeing these things, the centurion and his men hastened to Pilate by night, leaving the tomb they were watching, and narrated all things they had seen, fearing greatly, and saying: "Truly he was a Son of God" (ἀληθῶς υἱὸς ἦν θεοῦ). 46. Pilate answered and said, "I am pure of the blood of the Son of God, but thus it seemed good unto you" (ἐγὼ καθαρεύω τοῦ αἵματος τοῦ υἱοῦ τοῦ θεοῦ, ὑμῖν δὲ τοῦτο ἔδοξεν). 47. Then they all came to him beseeching and entreating him that he should command the centurion and the soldiers to say nothing of what they had seen, 48. "For it is better," they said, "to lay upon us the greatest sins before God, and not to fall into the hands of the people of the Jews and be

stoned." 49. Pilate, therefore, commanded the centurion and the soldiers to say nothing.

As the first Synoptic is the only Gospel which relates the story of the application to Pilate for a guard and the watch at the sepulchre, so of course it is the only one which gives the sequel to that episode; but this differs in every respect from the account in Peter. It is as follows (xxviii. 11 f.):

Some of the guard came into the city, and told unto the chief priests all the things that were come to pass. And when they were assembled with the elders, and had taken counsel, they gave large money unto the soldiers, saying, Say ye, His disciples came by night and stole him away while we slept. And if this come to the governor's ears, we will persuade him, and rid you of care. So they took the money, and did as they were taught: and this saying was spread abroad among the Jews, and continueth until this day.

When the centurion and soldiers in Peter go to Pilate after witnessing the events described as occurring at the resurrection, "fearing greatly" (ἀγωνιῶντες μεγάλως), they say, "Truly he was a Son of God" (ἀληθῶς υἱὸς ἦν θεοῦ). It will be remembered that, in the first Synoptic, when the centurion and they that were watching Jesus saw the earthquake and the things that were done when he expired, they "feared exceedingly" (ἐφοβήθησαν σφόδρα), and said, "Truly this was a Son of God" (ἀληθῶς θεοῦ υἱὸς ἦν οὗτος). The tradition of the astonished centurion bearing such testimony to Jesus is known to both writers, but under different circumstances, and independently treated. In similar fashion, the reply put into the mouth of Pilate in Peter, "I am pure of the blood (ἐγὼ καθαρεύω τοῦ αἵματος) of the Son of God, but thus it seemed good unto you," is, to a certain extent, the same as Pilate's declaration to the multitude after washing his hands (xxvii. 24 f.): "I am innocent of the blood of this righteous man (ἀθῷός εἰμι ἀπὸ τοῦ αἵματος τοῦ δικαίου τούτου): see ye to it;" but in this case, as well as the other, the details and the language show an independent use of a similar source. In the Synoptic, the centurion and soldiers do not go to Pilate at all, but are bribed by the chief priests and elders to say that his disciples stole him by night when they slept. They are warned by Pilate to be altogether silent, in Peter. As the desire of the author is represented to be to remove responsibility from Pilate and throw it all upon the Jews, it is difficult to conceive that, if he had this account before him, he could deliberately have left it unused, and preferred his own account.

We now come to the visit of the women to the sepulchre:

50. In the morning of the Lord's day, Mary Magdalene, a disciple of the Lord (through fear of the Jews, for they burnt with anger, she had not done at the grave of the Lord that which women are accustomed to do for those that die and are loved by them), 51. took her women friends with her and came to the grave where he was laid. 52. And they feared lest the Jews should see them, and said: "If we could not on that day on which he was crucified weep and lament, let us do these things even now at his grave. 53. But who will roll away the stone that is laid at the door of his grave (τίς δὲ ἀποκυλίσει ἡμῖν καὶ τὸν λίθον τὸν τεθέντα ἐπὶ τῆς θύρας τοῦ μνημείου) in order that we may enter and set ourselves by him and do the things that are due? 54. For great was the stone (μέγας γὰρ ἦν ὁ λίθος), and we fear lest some one should see us. And if we should not be able to do it, let us at least lay down before the door that which we bring in his memory, and let us weep and lament till we come to our home." 55. And they went and found the tomb opened and, coming near, they stooped down and see there a certain young man sitting in the midst of the tomb, beautiful and clad in a shining garment (καὶ προσελθοῦσαι παρέκυψαν ἐκεῖ, καὶ ὁρῶσιν ἐκεῖ τινα νεανίσκον καθεζόμενον μέσῳ τοῦ τάφου, ὡραῖον καὶ περιβεβλημένον στολὴν λαμπροτάτην), who said to them: 56. "Why are ye come? Whom seek ye? Him who was crucified? He

is risen and gone away. But if ye do not believe, stoop down and see the place where he lay, that he is not there; for he is risen and gone away whence he was sent" (τί ἤλθατε; τίνα ζητεῖτε; μὴ τὸν σταυρωθέντα ἐκεῖνον; ἀνέστη καὶ ἀπῆλθεν; εἰ δὲ μὴ πιστεύετε, παρακύψατε καὶ ἴδατε τὸν τόπον ἔνθα ἔκειτο, ὅτι οὐκ ἔστιν; ἀνέστη γὰρ καὶ ἀπῆλθεν ἐκεῖ ὅθεναρυ ἀπεστάλη). Then the women, frightened, fled.
We need not remark that in all essential points the account given here is different from that in our Gospels.

In each of the three Synoptics, it is said that the women saw where Jesus was laid, and the first two name Mary Magdalene and Mary the mother of Jesus (Mark "the other Mary"), Matt. xxvii. 61, Mark xv. 47, Luke xxiii. 55. All four canonical Gospels relate their coming to the sepulchre: Matthew (xxviii. 1), "late on the Sabbath day, as it began to dawn toward the first day of the week;" Mark (xvi. 1), "when the Sabbath was past;" Luke (xxiv. 1), "on the first day of the week at early dawn;" but only the second and third state that they bring spices to anoint Jesus; in Matthew the purpose stated being merely "to see the sepulchre." In the fourth Gospel, only Mary Magdalene comes, and no reason is assigned. In Peter, Mary Magdalene only is named, but she takes her women friends, and though spices are not directly named, they are distinctly implied, and the object of the visit to the tomb, admirably described as "that which women are accustomed to do for those who die and are loved by them," which they had not been able to do on the day of the crucifixion, through fear of the Jews. Even now the same fear is upon them; but nothing is said of it in the four Gospels.

The only part of the words put into their mouths by the author which at all corresponds with anything in the canonical narratives is that regarding the opening of the sepulchre. "But who will roll us away the stone that is laid at the door of the grave?" (τίς δὲ ἀποκυλίσει ἡμῖν καὶ τὸν λίθον τὸν τεθέντα, ἐπὶ τῆς θύρας τοῦ μνημείου?). In Matthew, an angel had rolled away the stone, but in Mark the women are represented as asking the same question among themselves (xvi. 3), "Who shall roll us away the stone from the door of the grave?" (τίς ἀποκυλίσει ἡμῖν τὸν λίθον ἐκ τῆς θύρας τοῦ μνημείου?) practically in the same words. To appreciate the relative importance of the similarity in this detail it should be remembered that the same words are used with slight grammatical changes in the other two Synoptics: Matt. xxviii. 2, the angel "rolled away the stone" (ἀπεκύλισε τὸν λίθον); and Luke xxiv. 2, they found "the stone rolled away from the grave" (τὸν λίθον ἀποκεκυλισμένον ἀπὸ τοῦ μνημείου). The privilege of using a similar source of tradition must also be accorded to the author of the fragment.

The women in Peter, after a few more words explanatory of their purpose in going to the sepulchre, use an expression to which so much importance has been attached by Zahn that, to render it intelligible, it must be connected with the context just discussed. "But who will roll away the stone that is laid at the door of the grave, in order that we may enter and set ourselves by him, and do the things that are due? For great was the stone (μέγας γὰρ ἦν ὁ λίθος), and we fear lest some one should see us." Now in the second Synoptic (xvi. 4) we read that the women, looking up, "see that the stone (λίθος) is rolled back; for it was exceeding great" (ἦν γὰρ μέγας σφόδρα). Zahn says: "Just as certainly can the dependence of the Gospel of Peter on Mark be proved. A proof scarcely to be refuted lies even in the one little word ἦν, which is mechanically taken from Mark xvi. 3."116 To one so willing to be convinced, what might not be proved by many little words in the canonical Gospels? It must be remembered that none of our Synoptics sprang full-fledged from the original tradition, but, as is recognised by every critic competent to form an opinion, is based on previous works and records of tradition, which gradually grew into this more complete form. Any one who wishes to realise this should examine

Rushbrooke's "Synopticon," which, at a glance, will show the matter and the language common to our first three Gospels, and leave little doubt as to the common origin of these works. It may be useful towards a proper understanding of the problem before us if we give a single illustration of the construction of the Synoptics taken from the very part of the narrative at which we have arrived. We shall arrange it in parallel columns for facility of comparison.

MATTHEW xxvii.	MARK xv.	LUKE xxiii.
55. And many women were there beholding from afar, which had followed Jesus from Galilee, ministering unto him: 56. among whom was Mary Magdalene, and Mary the mother of James and Joses, and the mother of the sons of Zebedee.	40. And there were also women beholding from afar: among whom were both Mary Magdalene and Mary the mother of James the less and of Joses, and Salome; 41. who, when he was in Galilee, followed him, and ministered unto him . . .	49. And all his acquaintance, and the women that followed him from Galilee, stood afar off, seeing these things. xxiv. 10. Now they were Mary Magdalene and Joanna, and Mary [the mother] of James, and other women with them. xxiii. 50.
57. And when even was come, there came a rich man from Arimathaea,	42. And when even was now come, . . . 43. there came Joseph of Arimathaea, a councillor of honourable estate,	50. And behold a man named Joseph, who was a councillor, a good man and a righteous, 51. . . . of Arimathaea, a city of the Jews,

MATTHEW xxvii.	MARK xv.	LUKE xxiii.
who also himself was Jesus' disciple:	who also himself was looking for the kingdom of God: and he boldly	who was looking for the kingdom of God:
58. this man went to Pilate, and asked for the body of Jesus.	went in unto Pilate and asked for the body of Jesus.	52. this man went to Pilate, and asked for the body of Jesus.

MATTHEW xxvii.	MARK xv.	LUKE xxiii.
55. Ἦσαν δὲ ἐκεῖ γυναῖκες πολλαὶ ἀπὸ μακρόθεν θεωροῦσαι, αἵτινες ἠκολούθησαν τῷ Ἰησοῦ ἀπὸ τῆς Γαλιλαίας διακονοῦσαι αὐτῷ, (56) ἐν αἷς ἦν Μαρία ἡ Μαγδαληνή, καὶ Μαρία ἡ τοῦ Ἰακώβου καὶ Ἰωσὴ μήτηρ, καὶ ἡ μήτηρ τῶν υἱῶν Ζεβεδαίου.	40. Ἦσαν δὲ καὶ γυναῖκες ἀπὸ μακρόθεν θεωροῦσαι, ἐν αἷς καὶ Μαρία ἡ Μαγδαληνὴ καὶ Μαρία ἡ Ἰακώβου τοῦ μικροῦ καὶ Ἰωσῆτος μήτηρ καὶ Σαλώμη, (41) αἳ ὅτε ἦν ἐν τῇ Γαλιλαίᾳ ἠκολούθουν αὐτῷ καὶ διηκόνουν αὐτῷ, . . .	49. Εἱστήκεισαν δὲ πάντες οἱ γνωστοὶ αὐτῷ ἀπὸ μακρόθεν, καὶ γυναῖκες αἱ συνακολουθοῦσαι αὐτῷ ἀπὸ τῆς Γαλιλαίας, ὁρῶσαι ταῦτα. (xxiv. 10) ἦσαν δὲ ἡ Μαγδαληνὴ Μαρία καὶ Ἰωάννα καὶ Μαρία ἡ Ἰακώβου καὶ αἱ λοιπαὶ σὺν αὐταῖς . . .
57. Ὀψίας δὲ γενομένης ἦλθεν ἄνθρωπος πλούσιος ἀπὸ Ἀριμαθαίας, τοὔνομα Ἰωσήφ,	42. καὶ ἤδη ὀψίας γενομένης, . . . (43) ἐλθὼν Ἰωσὴφ ἀπὸ Ἀριμαθαίας, εὐσχήμων βουλευτής, ὃς	50. Καὶ ἰδοὺ ἀνὴρ ὀνόματι Ἰωσὴφ βουλευτὴς ὑπάρχων, ἀνὴρ ἀγαθὸς καὶ δίκαιος, 51. . . . ἀπὸ Ἀριμαθαίας πόλεως τῶν Ἰουδαίων.
ὃς καὶ αὐτὸς ἐμαθητεύθη τῷ Ἰησοῦ · 58. οὗτος προσελθὼν τῷ Πειλάτῳ ᾐτήσατο τὸ σῶμα τοῦ Ἰησοῦ.	καὶ αὐτὸς ἦν προσδεχόμενος τὴν βασιλείαν τοῦ θεοῦ, τολμήσας εἰσῆλθεν πρὸς τὸν Πειλᾶτον καὶ ᾐτήσατο τὸ σῶμα τοῦ Ἰησοῦ.	ὃς προσεδέχετο τὴν βασιλείαν τοῦ θεοῦ. 52. οὗτος προσελθὼν τῷ Πειλάτῳ ᾐτήσατο τὸ σῶμα τοῦ Ἰησοῦ.

Or take, for instance, a few verses giving the arrest of Jesus as narrated by the three Synoptists:

MATTHEW xxvi.	MARK xiv.	LUKE xxii.
47. And while he yet spake, lo, Judas, one of the twelve, came, and with him a great multitude with swords and staves, from the chief priests and elders of the people.	43. And straightway, while he yet spake, cometh Judas, one of the twelve, and with him a multitude with swords and staves, from the chief priests and the scribes and the elders.	47. While he yet spake, lo, a multitude, and he that was called Judas, one of the twelve, went before them;
48. Now he that betrayed him gave them a sign, saying, Whomsoever I shall kiss, that is he: take him.	44. Now he that betrayed him had given them a token, saying, Whomsoever I shall kiss, that is he; take him, and lead him away safely.	and he drew near unto Jesus to kiss him.
49. And straightway he came to Jesus, and said, Hail, Rabbi; and kissed him.	45. And when he was come, straightway he came to him and saith, Rabbi; and kissed him.	

MATTHEW xxvi.	MARK xiv.	LUKE xxii.
50. And Jesus said unto him, Friend, do that for which thou art come. Then they came and laid hands on Jesus and took him.	46. And they laid hands on him and took him.	48. But Jesus said unto him, Judas, betrayest thou the Son of man with a kiss? (54. And they seized him and led him away.)
51. And lo, one of them that were with Jesus stretched out his hand, and drew his sword, and smote the servant of the high priest, and struck off his ear.	47. But a certain one of them that stood by drew his sword, and smote the servant of the high priest, and struck off his ear.	50. And a certain one of them smote the servant of the high priest, and struck off his right ear.
47. Καὶ ἔτι αὐτοῦ λαλοῦντος, ἰδοὺ Ἰούδας εἷς τῶν δώδεκα ἦλθεν, καὶ μετ' αὐτοῦ ὄχλος πολὺς μετὰ μαχαιρῶν καὶ ξύλων ἀπὸ τῶν ἀρχιερέων καὶ πρεσβυτέρων τοῦ λαοῦ.	43. Καὶ εὐθὺς ἔτι αὐτοῦ λαλοῦντος παραγίνεται Ἰούδας εἷς τῶν δώδεκα, καὶ μετ' αὐτοῦ ὄχλος μετὰ μαχαιρῶν καὶ ξύλων παρὰ τῶν ἀρχιερέων καὶ τῶν γραμματέων καὶ πρεσβυτέρων.	47. ἔτι αὐτοῦ λαλοῦντος, ἰδοὺ ὄχλος, καὶ ὁ λεγόμενος Ἰούδας εἷς τῶν δώδεκα προήρχετο αὐτούς, καὶ
48. ὁ δὲ παραδιδοὺς αὐτὸν ἔδωκεν αὐτοῖς σημεῖον λέγων· ὃν ἂν φιλήσω, αὐτός ἐστιν· κρατήσατε αὐτόν.	44. δεδώκει δὲ ὁ παραδιδοὺς αὐτὸν σύσσημον αὐτοῖς λέγων· ὃν ἂν φιλήσω, αὐτός ἐστιν· κρατήσατε αὐτὸν καὶ ἀπάγετε ἀσφαλῶς.	ἤγγισεν τῷ Ἰησοῦ φιλῆσαι αὐτόν.

49. Καὶ εὐθέως προσελθὼν τῷ Ἰησοῦ εἶπεν· χαῖρε ῥαββεί, καὶ κατεφίλησεν αὐτόν. 50. ὁ δὲ Ἰησοῦς εἶπεν αὐτῷ· ἑταῖρε, ἐφ' ὃ πάρει, τότε προσελθόντες ἐπέβαλον τὰς χεῖρας ἐπὶ τὸν Ἰησοῦν καὶ ἐκράτησαν αὐτόν. 51. Καὶ ἰδοὺ εἷς τῶν μετὰ Ἰησοῦ ἐκτείνας τὴν χεῖρα ἀπέσπασεν τὴν μάχαιραν αὐτοῦ, καὶ πατάξας τὸν δοῦλον τοῦ ἀρχιερέως ἀφεῖλεν αὐτοῦ τὸ ὠτίον.	45. Καὶ ἐλθὼν εὐθὺς προσελθὼν αὐτῷ λέγει· ῥαββεί, καὶ κατεφίλησεν αὐτόν. 46. οἱ δὲ ἐπέβαλαν τὰς χεῖρας αὐτῷ καὶ ἐκράτησαν αὐτόν. 47. εἷς δέ τις τῶν παρεστηκότων σπασάμενος τὴν μάχαιραν ἔπαισεν τὸν δοῦλον τοῦ ἀρχιερέως καὶ ἀφεῖλεν αὐτοῦ τὸ ὠτάριον.	48. Ἰησοῦς δὲ εἶπεν αὐτῷ· Ἰούδα, φιλήματι τὸν υἱὸν τοῦ ἀνθρώπου παραδίδως; (54. συλλαβόντες δὲ αὐτὸν ἤγαγον.) 50. καὶ ἐπάταξεν εἷς τις ἐξ αὐτῶν τοῦ ἀρχιερέως τὸν δοῦλον. καὶ ἀφεῖλεν τὸ οὖς αὐτοῦ τὸ δεξιόν.

Such close similarity as this, with occasional astonishing omissions of matter and flagrant contradictions where independent narrative is attempted, runs through the whole of the three Synoptics. This is not the place to enter upon any discussion of these phenomena, or any explanation of the origin of our Gospels, but apologists may be invited to consider the fact before passing judgment on the Gospel of Peter. Any coincidence of statement in the narrative of the fragment with any one of the four Gospels is promptly declared to be decisive evidence of dependence on that Gospel; and even the use of a word which has a parallel in them is sufficient reason for denouncing the author as a plagiarist. It would almost seem as if such critics had never read the prologue to the third Synoptic, and forgotten the πολλοί to which its author refers, when they limit the Christian tradition to these Gospels, which again, upon examination, must themselves be limited to two—the Synoptic and the Johannine, which in so great a degree contradict each other.

To return now to the passage which we have to examine. It will be observed that the second Synoptic treats the episode of the women in a manner different from the other two, but in the same style, though with very differing details, as Peter. We shall show reason for believing that both have drawn from the same source, but that the fragment has probably adhered more closely to the original source. In Mark (xvi. 3 f.) the women are, as in

Peter, represented as speaking: "And they were saying among themselves, 'Who shall roll us away the stone from the door of the tomb?'" Here the spoken words stop, and the writer continues to narrate: "And looking up, they see that the stone is rolled back (ἀνακεκύλισται): for it was (ἦν) exceeding great." It is obvious that the "was" here is quite out of place, and it seems impossible to avoid the conclusion that, originally, it must have stood with a different context. That different context we have in Peter. The women say amongst themselves: "Who will roll us away the stone that is laid at the door of the grave, in order that we may enter"—and, of course, in saying this they are supposed to have in their minds the stone which they had seen the evening before and, naturally, express their recollection of it in the past tense—"for it was exceeding great." If the phrase has been mechanically introduced, it has been so by the second Synoptist, in whose text it is more out of place than in Peter. A prescriptive right to early traditions of this kind cannot reasonably be claimed for any writer, simply because his compilation has happened to secure a place in the Canon.

When the women come to the tomb, they stoop down (παρέκυψαν) and see there (ὀρῶσιν ἐκεῖ) a certain young man (τινα νεανίσκον) sitting in the midst of the tomb, beautiful and clad in a shining garment (ὡραῖον καὶ περιβεβλημένον στολὴν λαμπροτάτην). This is the "certain man" who descended when the heavens were again opened, as described in v. 44. The realistic touch of the women stooping to look into the low entrance of the tomb is repeated when the "young man" bids them "stoop down" (παρακύψατε) and convince themselves that Jesus had risen. This does not occur in any of the Synoptics; but in the fourth Gospel (xx. 5), Peter, it is said, "stooping down" (παρακύψας) sees (βλέπει) the clothes. In Matthew, the angel sits upon the stone which he has rolled away, and not in the sepulchre, and his description is (xxviii. 3): "His appearance was as lightning, and his raiment white as snow" (ἦν δὲ ἡ εἰδέα αὐτοῦ ὡς ἀστραπὴ, καὶ τὸ ἔνδυμα αὐτοῦ λευκὸν ὡς χιών). In Mark (xvi. 8), they see a "young man" (νεανίσκον) sitting on the right side, and not in the middle, and he is "clad in a white robe" (περιβεβλημένον στολὴν λευκήν). In Luke (xxiv. 4), two men (ἄνδρες δύο) stand by the women "in dazzling apparel" (ἐν ἐσθῆτι ἀστραπτούσῃ). In the fourth Gospel (xx. 12), Mary sees two angels sitting, the one at the head, the other at the feet, where the body had lain, but they are simply said to be "in white" (ἐν λευκοῖς).

The "young man" says to the women in Peter: "Why are ye come? (τί ἤλθατε?) Whom seek ye? (τίνα ζητεῖτε?) Him who was crucified? (μὴ τὸν σταυρωθέντα ἐκεῖνον?) He is risen and gone away (ἀνέστη καὶ ἀπῆλθεν). But if ye do not believe, stoop down, and see the place where he lay (παρακύψατε καὶ ἴδατε τὸν τόπον ἔνθα ἔκειτο), that he is not there, for he is risen and gone away thither whence he was sent (ἀνέστη γὰρ καὶ ἀπῆλθεν ἐκεῖ ὅθεν ἀπεστάλη)." In Matthew (xxviii. 5 f.) the angel "answered and said unto the women" (who had not spoken to him, apparently) "Fear not ye: for I know that ye seek Jesus which hath been crucified (οἶδα γὰρ ὅτι Ἰησοῦν τὸν ἐσταυρωμένον ζητεῖτε). He is not here, for he rose (οὐκ ἔστιν ὧδε, ἠγέρθη γάρ), even as he said. Come, see the place where the Lord lay (δεῦτε ἴδετε τὸν τόπον ὅπου ἔκειτο). And go quickly, and tell his disciples he rose from the dead (ἠγέρθη ἀπὸ τῶν νεκρῶν); and lo, he goeth before you into Galilee; there shall ye see him: lo, I have told you." In Mark (xvi. 6 f.), this "young man" in the tomb says: "Be not amazed; ye seek Jesus the Nazarene which hath been crucified (Ἰησοῦν ζητεῖτε τὸν Ναζαρηνὸν τὸν ἐσταυρωμένον). He rose (ἠγέρθη); he is not here; behold, the place where they laid him! (οὐκ ἔστιν ὧδε; ἴδε ὁ τόπος ὅπου ἔθηκαν αὐτόν). But go tell his disciples and Peter, He goeth before you into Galilee: there shall ye see him, as he said unto you." The close resemblance of these two accounts in the first and second Gospels is striking, and scarcely less so is the resemblance, with important variations, of the third Synoptic (xxiv. 5 ff.). The "two men in dazzling apparel" say to the women, who stand with their faces bowed down towards the earth: "Why seek ye the living among the dead? He is not here, but he rose (οὐκ ἔστιν ὧδε, ἀλλὰ ἠγέρθη).117 Remember how he spake unto you when he was yet in Galilee, saying, that the Son of man must be delivered up into the hands of sinful men, and be crucified, and the third day rise again." The complete change in the reference to Galilee here will be observed.

The peculiar ending of the words of the "young man" in Peter is nowhere found in our Gospels: "He is risen and gone away thither whence he was sent." Mr. Robinson compares with this a passage from the 20th Homily of Aphrahat (ed. Wright, p. 385): "And the angel said to Mary, he is risen and gone away to him that sent him." Mr. Robinson adds: "There is reason to believe that Aphrahat, a Syrian writer, used Tatian's Harmony: and thus we seem to have a second link between our Gospel and that important work."118 But is it not rather a curious position in which to place the supposed "Diatessaron," to argue that a passage which it does not now contain was nevertheless in it because a Syrian writer who is supposed to have used the "Diatessaron" has quoted the passage? It shows how untrustworthy are all arguments regarding early works like the "Diatessaron." Looking at the other instances which could be pointed out, and to some of which we have referred, we see that everything not agreeing with the Gospels of the Church has been gradually eliminated or corrected into agreement, and that thus the very probable use of the Gospel according to Peter by Tatian may be concealed. As Mr. Robinson further points out, however, the words of the angel in Peter are in direct contradiction to those put into the mouth of Jesus in the fourth Gospel (xx. 17): "I am not yet ascended to the Father."

The conclusion of the whole episode in Peter is the short and comprehensive phrase: "Then the women, frightened, fled" (τότε αἱ γυναῖκες φοβηθεῖσαι ἔφυγον). In Matthew, in obedience to the order of the angel to go and tell his disciples, none of which is given in Peter, it is said (xxviii. 8): "And they departed quickly from the tomb with fear and great joy" (καὶ ἀπελθοῦσαι ταχὺ ἀπὸ τοῦ μνημείου μετὰ φόβου καὶ χαρᾶς μεγάλης), "and ran to bring his disciples word." In Mark (xvi. 8) it is said: "And they went out and fled from the tomb; for trembling and astonishment had come upon them (καὶ ἐξελθοῦσαι ἔφυγον ἀπὸ τοῦ μνημείου; εἶκεν γὰρ αὐτὰς τρόμος καί ἔκστασις). And they said nothing to anyone: for they were afraid" (ἐφοβοῦντο γάρ). The running to bring the disciples word, in the first, and the saying nothing to any one, of the second, Synoptic, is a case of curious contradiction in details. The third Gospel twice over repeats the statement that the women told what they had heard "to the eleven and to all the rest" (xxiv. 9, 10), but says nothing of the emotions excited by the interview, except the double statement (xxiv. 8), "And they remembered his words," and, 11, "And these words appeared in their sight as idle talk, and they disbelieved them."

In the first Synoptic, however (xxviii. 9 f.), as the women go, the risen Jesus himself meets them and delivers the same order to tell the disciples to depart into Galilee, where they shall see him. The genuine portion of the second Synoptic ends with the words quoted above, and it is only in the added conclusion (xvi. 9. 20) that we meet with an account of an appearance to Mary Magdalene in the morning. The third Synoptic relates no appearance to the women or any one that morning; but the fourth Gospel has the appearance of Jesus to Mary Magdalene, and a long interview between them. Now all this is quite distinctly excluded from the Gospel according to Peter, and those who argue for the dependence of the work on our Gospels have to explain this deliberate omission.

The fragment proceeds:

58. And it was the last day of the Unleavened bread, and many went forth, returning to their homes, the feast being ended. 59. But we, the twelve disciples of the Lord, wept and mourned, and each went to his home sorrowing for that which had happened. 60. But I, Simon Peter, and Andrew, my brother, took our nets and went to the sea, and there was with us Levi, the son of Alphaeus, whom the Lord....

And so, at a most interesting point, the fragment breaks off, in the middle of a phrase. This, it will be observed, distinctly excludes the vision to the two disciples in the country, mentioned Mark xvi. 12 f., supposing it to be that described in the third Synoptic (xxiv. 13 ff.), of which long narrative no hint is given in Peter. It also, of course, excludes the appearance to the disciples in the room, described in the fourth Gospel (xix. 20 ff.), and the breathing of the Holy Ghost upon them, of which very important episode the three Synoptics are equally ignorant, as well as the second appearance to them and the conviction of the unbelieving Thomas, which only this Gospel records. We may add that the appearance to the eleven as they sat at meat, related in the addition to the second Synoptic (xvi. 14 f.), with the mission of the apostles "into all the world," with miraculous powers endowed, which the other Gospels do not mention, is likewise excluded by Peter.

This is not all that is excluded, however, for in the fragment reference is distinctly made to the "twelve disciples," which is an explicit confirmation of the statement made in v. 26 f., "I and my companions ... were fasting and mourning," which makes no exception any more than the similar "We, the twelve disciples of the Lord" now quoted. Supposing this statement to be deliberately made, and we have no reason whatever from anything in the rest of the fragment to doubt it, this completely excludes the whole of the story of a betrayal of his master by Judas Iscariot.

Various facts must be remembered in confirmation of the view that the "betrayal" of Jesus by Judas Iscariot was unknown to the older tradition. In the Apocalypse (xxi. 14) it is said that upon the twelve foundations of the Holy City, the New Jerusalem, are written "the twelve names of the twelve apostles of the Lamb." If, as is generally believed, this Apocalypse was written by John the Apostle, is it possible that, if Judas had betrayed his master in the manner described by the canonical Gospels, he could deliberately have written this, using twice over the "twelve," which includes that Apostle? Again, in the first epistle to the Corinthians (i. xv. 5), in relating the supposed "appearances" of Jesus, it is said that he first appeared to Cephas: "Then unto the twelve."119 If the point be considered on the mere ground of historical probability, there is every reason to consider that the betrayal by Judas is a later product of the "evolved gnosis." Jesus is described as going about everywhere with his disciples, and nothing could have been easier, under the circumstances, than to follow and quietly arrest him, without any betrayal at all. In fact, there is no real need shown for such a betrayal, and the older Christian tradition probably did not contain it. It was just the trait which the "evolved gnosis" would add to the picture from such a passage as Psalm xli. 9: "Yea, mine own familiar friend, in whom I trusted, which did eat of my bread, hath lifted up his heel against me," and which was given its literal fulfilment in the detail mentioned in the first and second Synoptics (Matt. xxvi. 23, Mark. xiv. 20), "He that dipped his hand with me in the dish, the same shall betray me." It may be mentioned that Justin does not appear to have known anything of a betrayal of Jesus, and that, in places where, if he had been aware of the episode, he would certainly have referred to it, he passes over it in total silence.

According to the fragment, Simon Peter, and at least some of the disciples, must have gone into Galilee without any vision of the risen Jesus; and probably the last verse, which is broken off so abruptly, prepares the account of such an appearance as is described in the much-questioned last chapter of the fourth Gospel. It is worth pointing out, as perhaps an indication of the tradition which Peter follows, that both in the first and second Synoptic the order is given to the disciples to go into Galilee, where they are told that they are to see Jesus. In spite of this distinct order and statement, the author of the first Synoptic describes Jesus as immediately after appearing to the women, and giving the same direction to go into Galilee (xxviii. 7, 10), whilst in the spurious verses of Mark he nevertheless appears in Jerusalem to Mary Magdalene and to the Apostles. The third Synoptist gives a different turn to the mention of Galilee; but after the direction to go into Galilee, there to see Jesus, the visions described are a mere afterthought. In Peter, without any order, the disciples apparently go to Galilee, and there probably would be placed the first vision of the risen Jesus.

IX

We have now completed our comparison of the fragment with the canonical Gospels, and are able to form some opinion of its relative antiquity and relationship to our Gospels. Is it, as apologetic critics assert, a mere compilation from them, or can it take an independent position beside them, as a work derived from similar sources, and giving its own version of early Christian tradition? We have shown that it is not a compilation from our Gospels, but presents unmistakable signs of being an independent composition, and consequently a most interesting representation of Christian thought during the period when our Synoptic Gospels were likewise giving definite shape to the same traditions. Every part of this fragment has been set side by side with the corresponding narrative in the canonical Gospels, and it is simply surprising that a writing, dealing with a similar epoch of the same story, should have shown such freedom of handling. That there should be some correspondence between them was inevitable, but the wonder is not that there should be so much agreement, but so much divergence; and this wonder increases in proportion as a later date is assigned to the fragment, and the authority of the canonical Gospels had become more established.

The theory of "tendency" was sure to be advanced as an explanation of differences of treatment of the same story, but this seems to us much exaggerated in what is said of the Gospel according to Peter. That early Docetic views might be supposed to be favoured by its representations is very possible; but these are far from being so pronounced as to render it unacceptable to those not holding such opinions, and the manner in which Justin and Origen make use of its statements is proof of this. As to its anti-Judaistic tone, a certain distinction has to be drawn. The expressions regarding "the Jews," "their feast" (used in reference to the Passover), and so on, may be put in the same category as the definition of the veil of the Temple "of Jerusalem," as indicating merely a work probably written out of Judaea, and for Gentile Christians; but in throwing upon the Jews, much more than on the Roman power, the odium of having crucified Jesus, the difference between Peter and the canonical Gospels is really infinitesimal. He certainly represents Pilate as retiring early from the trial, and leaving it to Herod, in whose "jurisdiction" it was, after washing his hands of the whole business; but this is a much more probable account, and perhaps an earlier tradition, than that which makes a Roman governor present the incredible and humiliating spectacle of a judge condemning and crucifying a man, in whom he finds no fault, at the dictation of a Jewish mob. The canonical Gospels, however, only accentuate the guilt of the Jews by representing the chief priests and elders, as well as the multitude, obstinately clamouring for his crucifixion, and finally overcoming Pilate's scruples. It is the chief priests and rulers who first seize Jesus and plot for his betrayal, who spit in his face, buffet and mock him, who prefer to him Barabbas, and cry: "His blood be on us and on our children" (Matt. xxvii. 25). The expressions of distinct antagonism to the Jews in the fourth Gospel far exceed any in the Gospel according to Peter. There is, therefore, no preconceived purpose conceivable to account for the characteristics of the narrative in this fragment.

That a writer who had our canonical Gospels before him should so depart from their lines, alter every representation without dogmatic purpose, insert contradictory statements, and omit episodes of absorbing interest and passages which would have enriched his narrative, is a theory which cannot be established. It is obvious that the feeling of the writer is one of intense devotion and reverence, and it is unreasonable to suppose that he could have passed over, altered, and contradicted so many points in the narrative of the Gospels, had he had those works before him.120 In all probability he composed his work from earlier records and traditions, of the existence of which we have evidence in Luke i. 1, and the degree of resemblance on the one hand, and of discrepancy on the other, proceeds from independent use of these sources, from which the materials used in the canonical Gospels may have been drawn. It had not the good fortune of these Gospels, however, to be adopted by the Church and subjected, like them, to repeated revisal; but, drifting apart on the stream of time, it at last comes to us with all its original sins and imperfections on its head. Of course, any judgment now formed on the Gospel according to Peter is subject to the unfortunate limitation that we have only a fragment of the work in our hands; but should the rest be discovered, as we hope, it will not affect conclusions now based upon the part before us, whatever may be the final verdict on the whole.

X

We have still to consider objections raised by Mr. Rendel Harris, however, concerning the relation between this fragment and the Gospels accepted by the Church. In a long article in the "Contemporary Review" he tries to establish the thesis that "The Gospel of Peter shows everywhere the traces of a highly evolved prophetic gnosis, and in particular most of the apparently new matter which it contains is taken from the Old Testament."121 It would not be possible, without wearying the most patient of parishioners, to illustrate in any adequate manner the perverse and hair-splitting ingenuity with which the "highly evolved prophetic gnosis" went to work, and which, in very parlous fashion, Mr. Harris applies to Peter; but, fortunately, this will not be necessary here. This gnosis doubtless began its operation early, and reached a climax towards the fourth century; but then it had ceased to be creative, and had become wildly analytical. Nothing then remained for it to do. Mr. Rendel Harris quotes, with admirable courage, a "significant sentence" from the "Peregrinatio ad Loca Sancta," a work of St. Sylvia of Aquitaine, or some other lady traveller of the fourth century, which has recently been published. She has been relating how the people were instructed in the mysteries of the faith by readings from the Scriptures, imprimis; of the Psalms predictive of the Messianic sufferings; then of passages from the Acts and Epistles which bear upon the interpretation of such predictions; further, the evidence of the prophets; and, to crown all, the story of the Passion itself from the Gospels. "The object of this service was, as Sylvia points out, that the people might understand by the Gospel record that whatever the psalmists and prophets had foretold concerning the Passion of the Lord had actually taken place." And now comes the "significant sentence" to which we referred above, italicised by Mr. Harris himself: "And so for the space of three hours the people is taught that nothing took place which had not been previously foretold, and nothing had been foretold which had not obtained its fulfilment." Mr. Harris supports the accuracy of Sylvia's description.122

But, whilst frankly admitting the application of this fundamental principle of the prophetic gnosis, more or less throughout all early Christian literature, Mr. Harris wishes to limit its influence upon works received into the canon, into which the two-edged weapon, however, pierces in spite of him to the sundering apart of soul and body. He says:

Now no history is, in its ultimate analysis, so trustworthy as Christian history, but if we take the whole body of early literature, of which the canonical Gospels form the centre and crown, including Apocalypses, party-gospels, and the like, we shall find that there never was a body of history which was so overgrown with legend, and the major part of these legends result from the irregular study of the Old Testament, probably based on the synagogue methods of the time of the early Christian teachers. This reaction of the prophecy upon history colours the style of authors and affects their statements; and it is only by a close and careful study of the writers and their methods, that we are able to discriminate between what is a bona fide allusion in the Prophets, or what is a trick of style borrowed from the Prophets, or what is a pure legend invented out of the Prophets.123

The immediate object here, of course, is to lay the basis of an indictment against the fragment; but in this clear and excellent statement, a principle is enunciated, the application of which cannot be directed as the writer pleases, but is apt to be as deadly to friends as to foes. Mr. Harris may attempt to satisfy his doubts, in writing with the impartiality of a scholar, as he does, with the reservation that "no history is, in its ultimate analysis, so trustworthy as Christian history," but he has only to formulate the reasons for such a statement, to recognise their utter inadequacy. In so far as he gives us any glimpse of them here, they are of sad insufficiency. He speaks, a little further on, regarding "the real need of a critical method that can distinguish between statements that are genuine history, and statements that are prophetic reflexes. For this discrimination," he says, "our main guide is the Canon, which expresses the judgment of the primitive Christian Church upon its literary materials; but I think it will be generally felt that we shall need finer-edged tools than Church customs or decrees in the more difficult parts of the problem; and certainly we must not assume a priori in a critical investigation, that there is no trace of legendary accretion in the Gospel, and no element of genuine fact in what are called the Apocrypha."124 Alas! is not the "main guide" a mere blind leader of the blind in regard to "the encroachment of prophetic interpretation upon the historical record"? We have no intention of maintaining here a very different view of the credibility of Christian history, the arguments against which we have elsewhere fully stated, but it is desirable, for reasons which will presently appear, that the fundamental principle of this attack on the Gospel according to Peter should be clearly understood. Mr. Harris goes on to affirm that the measure of this encroachment is, in the first two centuries, one of the best indications of documentary date we possess: "As a test, it will settle the period of many a document, and perhaps the measure of the appeal to prophecy will even determine the chronological order of the Gospels themselves: Mark, Luke, John, and Matthew."125 This order will probably surprise a good many readers, and shake the faith they might perhaps be disposed to repose in the test which is supposed to have decided it. Mr. Harris applies the test in various instances to Peter, and we shall briefly examine his results.

It will be remembered that in v. 35 f. whilst the soldiers were keeping watch over the sepulchre, there was a great voice in the heavens, and they saw the heavens opened, and "two men" (δύο ἄνδρας) came down from thence with great light, and approach the tomb, and the stone which had been laid at the door rolled away, and they entered it, but presently they beheld again three men (τρεῖς ἄνδρας) coming out, and the two were supporting or conducting the other by the hand, and the lofty stature of the three is described. Now the "highly evolved prophetic gnosis" by which, according to Mr. Harris, this representation was composed is as follows, though only the main lines of the painful process can be given. In the prayer of Habakkuk (iii. 2), according to the Septuagint, the words which stand in our Bible, "In the midst of the years make known" reads: "In the midst of two lives" (or of two living creatures) "thou shalt be known." This is referred in two ways: to "Christ's incarnation" and to his "Death and Resurrection." In the former case the two animals are the ox and the ass at the Nativity. The interpretation in the second case: the "living creatures" are the seraphim, two in number, because in Isaiah (vi. 3) "one called to the other and said:" "and we have only to find a situation in which Christ is seen between two angels, and the prophecy is fulfilled. This situation is made in the Gospel of Peter by Christ rising between two supporting angels." Mr. Harris endeavours to strengthen this by referring to Cyril of Alexandria's comment on the two living creatures (in the fourth century). Cyril is in doubt whether the two living creatures are the Father and the Holy Spirit, or the Old and New Testament, but recurs to the earlier interpretation that they are the Cherubim. Mr. Harris also cites the Targum of Jonathan Ben Uzziel on Zechariah iii. 7: "If thou wilt keep the observation of my word, I will raise thee up in the resurrection of the dead, and set thy feet walking between the two cherubim." Then, as soon as this identification of the two living creatures had been made, it was easy, says Mr. Harris, to pass over to the ninety-ninth Psalm, which Justin[126] affirms to be a prediction of Christ.

A little study of the opening words will show some interesting parallels with Peter. "The Lord hath reigned! Let the people be enraged! Sitting on the Cherubim, let the earth be shaken. The Lord in Zion is great and high above all the people." Here we have a parallel to the "Jews burning with rage," and to the enormous stature of the risen Christ, and, perhaps to the quaking of the earth. Nor is it without interest that Justin, having spoken of this great and high Christ, should turn immediately to another Psalm (xix.) where the sun is said to come forth as a bridegroom from his chamber, and to rejoice as a giant to run a race.127

In order to be as just as possible, all this has been given in greater detail than perhaps the case deserves. It seems rather a heavy avalanche of conjecture to bring down upon Peter, who simply narrates, without the most distant reference to any prophetic texts; and it is perhaps a little hard that Justin, who in all probability had the Gospel already written and before him, should contribute in this casual way to the author's discomfiture. However, let us see what there is to be said upon the other side. The first general remark that may be made is, that it can scarcely be considered evidence of the later date of Peter to ascribe to him, as the source of this detail, an elaborate twisting of texts through the operation of gnosis, which has not been proved to have existed in this form before the epoch at which he wrote. This is said without any intention of casting doubt on the general operation of supposed prophetic passages on the evolution of Gospel history, but merely as questioning this particular explanation of the mode in which this representation was originally suggested, and more especially for the purpose of adding that, whatever reproach of this kind is cast upon the Gospel according to Peter, must equally be directed against the canonical gospels.

It will be remembered that, in the third Synoptic, "two men in shining apparel" assist at the resurrection, and that in the fourth Gospel Mary sees in the tomb "two angels in white sitting, the one at the head, the other at the feet, where the body of Jesus had lain." Here there is an occasion for applying with equal—or, as we shall presently see, greater—propriety the argument of "highly evolved prophetic gnosis" to the writers, and so explaining their representation. But there is more to be suggested in connection with the matter. In the first and second Synoptics, only one angel assists at the scene, who in the second Synoptic is called "a young man" (νεανίσκος). Now the "two men" of great stature in Peter only go into the tomb and come out again with Jesus; but subsequently the heavens were again opened (v. 44), and a certain man descends and goes into the tomb and remains there, for when the women come (v. 55) they see there "a certain young man" (νεανίσκος) "sitting in the midst of the tomb, beautiful and clad in a shining garment," who speaks to them as in the two Synoptics, and tells them that "Jesus is gone thither whence he was sent." This, then, is the angel who appears in Matthew and Mark. We have already mentioned that the two men of v. 36 have been identified by some critics as Moses and Elias. The account of the transfiguration is given in all the Synoptics, though it does not seem to have been known to the author of the fourth Gospel—although "John" was an actor in the scene—but that in the third Synoptic is fuller than the rest (ix. 28 ff). Jesus takes with him Peter and John and James, and goes up into the mountain to pray; and as he prays his countenance was altered, and his raiment becomes white and dazzling; "and behold there talked with him two men (ἄνδρες δύο), which were Moses and Elijah; who appeared in glory, and spake of his decease which he was about to accomplish at Jerusalem." When Peter and the others were fully awake, "they saw his glory and the two men (δύο ἄνδρας) that stood with him. And it came to pass, as they were parting from him, Peter said unto Jesus, Master, it is good for us to be here; and let us make three tabernacles; one for thee, and one for Moses, and one for Elijah: not knowing what he said. And while he said these things there came a cloud, and overshadowed them ... and a voice came out of the cloud, saying, This is my son, my chosen: hear ye him." To this episode Mr. Harris might reasonably apply the test of the "highly evolved prophetic gnosis;" but in any case, the view that the two men of the fragment are intended to represent Moses and Elijah—the law and the prophets—who had so short a time before "spoken of his decease which he was about to accomplish in Jerusalem," and who now came, in stature reaching to the heavens, but less than his which rose above the heavens, and conducted Jesus the Christ forth from the tomb, in which that decease had been fulfilled, is in the highest degree probable. Much more might be said regarding this, but too much time has already been devoted to the point.

The second application of Mr. Harris's test is to the sealing of the stone at the sepulchre with seven seals. The Gospel of Peter simply states that the stone was sealed with seven seals, and Mr. Harris endeavours to find some abstruse meaning in the statement, which is peculiar to the fragment in so far as the number of seals is concerned. Where did Peter get the idea? Mr. Harris says, first from Zechariah iii. 9: "For behold the stone that I have set before Joshua; upon one stone are seven eyes; behold I will engrave the graving thereof, saith the Lord of hosts;" and the name Joshua is the Hebrew equivalent of Jesus. A reference is also made by the Fathers of the second century to passages to prove that Christ was the stone (of stumbling to the Jews, but the corner stone to believers). "Justin recognised Christ in the stone cut out without hands, of which Daniel speaks; in the stone which Jacob set for his pillow, and which he anointed with oil; in the stone on which Moses sat in the battle with Amalek," and the like. "Bearing in mind that there was an early tendency to connect the language of the 'Branch' passage with the resurrection, we can see that the interpretation took a second form, viz. to regard the stone before the face of Jesus as a prophecy of the stone which closed the tomb in the evangelic story." There is evidence, Mr. Harris says, that the seven eyes were early interpreted by Biblical Targumists to mean seven seals.

We need not be surprised, then, that the Peter Gospel speaks of the stone as sealed with seven seals; it is an attempt to throw the story into closer parallelism with Zechariah, no doubt for polemic purposes against the Jews. That he uses the curious word ἐπέχρισαν, which we are obliged, from the exigencies of language, to translate "they smeared" or "plastered" seven seals, but which to the writer meant much the same as if he were to say, "they on-christed seven seals," is due to the lurking desire to make a parallel with Christ and the stone directly, and with the anointed pillar of Jacob. The stone has a chrism.... But this is not all; in Zechariah (iv. 10) there is a passage, "they shall see the plummet in the hand of Zerubbabel," but in the Septuagint it runs, "they shall see the tin-stone." How is this to be connected with the "stone before the face of Joshua or Jesus"? The answer is found in the pages of the Peter Gospel: "a great crowd came from Jerusalem and the neighbourhood to see the tomb which had been sealed." It only remains to identify the stone which they saw with the tin-stone. Symmachus retranslated the Hebrew word for "tin" as if it came from the root which means "to separate or divide," and in the Gospel of Peter, "the stone which had been laid on the door of the tomb withdrew (or separated) gradually" (ἐπεχώρησε παρὰ μέρος).
"The 'plummet' of Zerubbabel," Mr. Harris triumphantly concludes, "is used by Peter to make history square with prophecy."128

Now again the general remark has to be made that, in order to convict Peter of a late date, Mr. Harris takes all this "highly evolved gnosis" wherever he can find it, without consideration of epochs, and in some parts upon mere personal conjecture. He even confesses that he does not know the date of the translation of Symmachus, which he nevertheless uses as an argument. He observes, himself, that it is "a little awkward" that the stone, which at one time represents Jesus, has to be treated in the same breath as before the face of Jesus. The terribly complicated and involved process, by which it is suggested that the author of the Gospel according to Peter evolved a detail so apparently simple as the sealing of the sepulchre with seven seals, is difficult enough to follow, and must have been still more difficult to invent, but in his anxiety to assign a late date to the fragment, Mr. Harris forgets that, if the number seven is evidence of it, a large part of the New Testament must be moved back with the fragment. The Synoptics are full of it,[129] but it is quite sufficient to point to the Apocalypse, which has this typical number in almost every chapter: the message to the seven churches; the seven spirits before the throne; the seven golden candlesticks; the seven stars; seven lamps of fire burning; seven angels; seven trumpets; seven thunders; the dragon with seven heads, and seven diadems; the seven angels with seven plagues; the woman with seven heads, and so on. The most striking and apposite instance, which Mr. Harris indeed does not pass over, but mentions as having "a curious and suggestive connection" and "every appearance of being ultimately derived from the language of Zechariah,"[130] is the Book which is close sealed with seven seals, and the Lamb standing as though it had been slain, having seven horns and seven eyes, which are seven spirits of God, which is found worthy to take the book and open the seals.[131] Instead of giving the author of the fragment, who does not make the slightest claim to it, credit for so extraordinary a feat of synthetic exegesis, is it not more simple and probable that he used the number seven as a mere ordinary symbol of completeness? but if more than this be deemed requisite, and the detail has a deeper mystical sense, he can only be accused of "highly evolved prophetic gnosis," in company with the author of the Apocalypse and other canonical books, and this still gives him a position in the same epoch with them, more than which, probably, no one demands.

Another instance may be rapidly disposed of. The writer of Peter, Mr. Harris affirms, was not ignorant of the gnosis of the Cross wrought out by the Fathers from the Old Testament, on the "Wood" and the "Tree." One passage at which they laboured heavily is in Habakkuk ii. 11: "The stone cries out of the wall, and the cross-beam answers back to it." Mr. Harris proceeds:

Now the author of the Peter Gospel has been at work on the passage; he wishes to make the cross talk, and not only talk, but answer back; accordingly, he introduces a question: "Hast thou preached to them that are asleep?" and the response is heard from the cross, "Yea." As far as I can suspect, the first speaker is Christ, the Stone; and the answer comes from the Cross, the Wood. It is then the Cross that has descended into Hades. But perhaps this is pressing the writer's words a little too far.132 Is it not also pressing the writer's thoughts a little too far to suggest such trains of childish interpretation as the origin of all his characteristic representations? Mr. Harris, by way of bringing the charge nearer to Peter, says that the passage of Habakkuk "is quoted by Barnabas, though no doubt from a corrupted text, with a positive assertion that the Cross is here intimated by the prophet."133 This is not so. The passage in Barnabas (xii.) reads: "He defineth concerning the Cross in another prophet, who saith: 'And when shall these things be accomplished? saith the Lord. Whensoever a tree shall be bended and stand upright, and whensoever blood shall drop from a tree.' Again thou art taught concerning the cross and him that was to be crucified." This is not a quotation from Habakkuk, but from 4 Esdras v. 5. This is, however, not of much importance. It is of greater moment to observe that Mr. Harris, in applying this test, is only able to "suspect" that, in this episode in Peter, the speaker who asks the question is Christ the "stone," and the answer from the cross, the "wood;" but as the first "speaker" is a voice "out of the heavens," it is difficult to connect it with "Christ the Stone," to whom the question is actually addressed. According to this, he puts the question to himself. Such exegesis, applied to almost any conceivable statement, might prove almost any conceivable hypothesis.

The next instance requires us to turn to a passage in Amos (viii. 9-10, LXX): "And it shall come to pass in that day, saith the Lord God, that the sun shall set at midday, ... and I will turn your feasts into wailing and all your songs to lamentation, and I will lay sackcloth on all loins, and baldness on every head; and I will set him as the wailing for the beloved, and those that are with him as a day of grief." With it, we are told, must be taken the parallel verse in which Zechariah (xiv. 6, 7) predicts a day in which "there shall be no light, but cold and frost ... but towards evening there shall be light." This was one of the proofs with early Christians of the events which happened at the crucifixion, and St. Cyprian, for instance, quotes it. It is also quoted in the sixth Homily of the Persian Father Aphrahat against the Jews. "The Gospel of Peter did not apparently possess the gnosis in such a highly evolved form as this," but works on the same lines. Mr. Harris then quotes passages from the fragment, which we shall give after him, with his inserted comments, but as he does not mark the intervals which occur between them, we shall take the liberty of inserting the verses from which they are taken between brackets.

15. It was mid-day and darkness over all the land of Judaea.... 22. then the sun shone out, and it was found to be the ninth hour [at evening time it shall be light]; 23. and the Jews rejoiced.... 25. and the Jews began to wail [I will turn your feasts into mourning].... 26. We also were fasting and sitting down (i.e.sitting on the ground in sackcloth134); [I will lay sackcloth on all loins]. 50. Mary Magdalene had not done at the tomb as

women are wont to do over their dead beloveds, so she took her friends with her to wail [I will set him as the Wailing for the Beloved].

The writer is, therefore, drawing on the details of prophecy, as suggested by the current testimonies against the Jews, and most likely on a written gnosis involving these testimonies. That he veils his sources simply shows that he is not one of the first brood of anti-Jewish preachers. If he had been early, he would not have been artificial or occult.135

Now, as before, Mr. Harris uses the eccentricities of a gnosis which he does not prove to have existed at the time the fragment may have been written and, for instance, he quotes St. Cyprian, who wrote in the second half of the third century, and the Persian Father Aphrahat, also a writer long after the Gospel of Peter was composed, and his remark that the writer "did not apparently possess the gnosis in so highly evolved a form" as Aphrahat, is not so much an admission in his favour as to prepare the reader to be content with inferior evidence. The test, however, quite as much applies to our Gospels as to the Gospel of Peter. In the previous working, of which the fragment says nothing, those who pass "wag their heads" and rail, in each of the Synoptics, in a jubilant way. The first Synoptic says (xxvii. 45 f.) "Now from the sixth hour there was darkness over all the land until the ninth hour." The centurion and those who were watching "feared exceedingly." In Mark (xv. 33) there also "was darkness over the whole earth until the ninth hour," but in Luke (xxiii. 44 f.) the resemblance is still more marked. The darkness comes over the whole earth from the sixth until the ninth hour, "the sun's light failing." (48) "And all the multitudes that came together to this sight, when they beheld the things that were done, returned smiting their breasts." In the fourth Gospel (xx. 11), Mary goes to the tomb weeping. We shall have more to say regarding the Gospels presently, but here we need only remark that, whether in exactly the same way or not, the "highly evolved prophetic gnosis" has certainly done its work in all of them. In this respect, the Gospel of Peter merely takes its place with the rest.

There is only one other instance to be noticed here. It refers to some of the details which the writer of the fragment introduces into the mockery which precedes the crucifixion. Some of the mockers "prick" Jesus with a reed; others spat on his eyes. This, Mr. Harris says, is connected with a view early taken regarding a change of Jewish feasts. In the Epistle of Barnabas, there is the best exposition of the doctrine that the Feast should be turned into mourning and the Passover at which Jesus suffered should be treated as if it had been the Day of Atonement. In Barnabas, the ritual of the great day is discussed in detail, and the rules of procedure for the Priests and the People, apparently taken, Mr. Harris thinks, from a Greek handbook, prove a variety of local usage such as would not have been suspected from the Scripture, read apart from the rest of the literature of the time. The "unwashed inwards" of one goat, offered at the fast for all sins, are to be eaten by the priests alone, with vinegar, while the people fast and wail in sackcloth and ashes. This goat is one of two over which lot is cast on the Day of Atonement; the other is the scape-goat, Azazel, which, according to Barnabas, was to be treated with contumely, and sent away into the wilderness: "All of you spit on him, and prick him, and put the scarlet wool on his head," &c. Now the two goats both represent Christ, according to Barnabas, "who twists these written regulations into prophecies of the first and second Advents, and of the details of the Passion."

The mention of vinegar to be eaten with the bitter portion of the goat, suggested the words of the Psalm: "Gall for my meat and vinegar for my drink;" the command to spit on the goat and prick (or pierce) him [which ill-usage, by the way, the Talmud

admits to have been the practice of the Alexandrian Jews], is interpreted by Barnabas to be a type or a prophecy of Christ "set at naught and pierced and spat on." Is there any trace of the gnosis of the two goats in Peter? If we may judge from the conjunction of the words in the account of the Mockery, there is a decided trace: "Others stood and spat on his eyes ... others pricked him with a reed;" it is Christ as the goat Azazel.
Mr. Harris quotes "an almost contemporary Sibyllist," "They shall prick his side with a reed, according to their law;" and he continues: "If the Sybillist is quoting Peter, he is also interpreting him, and his interpretation is, they shall prick him, as is done to the goat Azazel."

To make Peter responsible for the ideas or interpretations of the Sybillist is a little hard. However, let us examine this matter. It is to be observed that the only innovation in Peter, regarding the spitting, is the expression that they "spat upon his eyes" instead of simply "upon him," or "in his face," as in the Gospels; but upon this nothing turns. The point is not even mentioned; so it may be dismissed. Regarding the reed, Peter says they "pierced" him with it, instead of "smote him" with it. Let us leave the "piercing" aside for the moment. In all other respects, the contumely is the same in the Gospels. Before the high priest, in Matthew and Mark (Matt. xxvi. 67, Mark xiv. 65), they spit in his face and buffet him, and smite him with the palms of their hands; and in Luke (xxii. 63 f.) they mock and beat him and revile him. It is curious that, according to the second Synoptist, all this was foretold, for he makes Jesus say (x. 33 f.): "Behold, we go up to Jerusalem; and the Son of man shall be delivered unto the chief priests and the scribes: and they shall condemn him to death, and shall deliver him unto the Gentiles: and they shall mock him, and shall spit upon him, and shall scourge him, and shall kill him, and after three days he shall rise again." After the trial before Pilate, in Mark (xv. 17 ff.), they put on him a purple robe, and the crown of thorns on his head, and a reed in his hand, and spit upon him, and take the reed and smite him on the head. In Peter, likewise, they clothe him in purple, put on his head the crown of thorns, spit upon his eyes, smite him on the cheeks, and pierce him with a reed.

What difference is there here except the mere piercing? Yes! there is a difference, for Mr. Harris has forgotten to refer to the scarlet wool put on the goat Azazel. There is nothing in Peter which corresponds with the scarlet wool. The robe that is put upon Jesus is purple. Now Barnabas, in the chapter from which Mr. Harris quotes all these passages, finds this point of the "scarlet wool" fulfilled in Jesus: "For they shall see him in that day wearing the long scarlet robe about his flesh."136 But if we look in the first Synoptic we also find this, for we read (xxvii. 28): "And they stripped him, and put on him a scarlet robe" (χλαμύδα κοκκίνην). The mere detail of piercing with the reed instead of smiting with it is trifling compared with this, and in all essential points Mr. Harris's test more fitly applies to the first Synoptic than to Peter, and equally so to the other two.

As for the piercing with the reed, however, we have only to turn to the fourth Gospel, and we find its counterpart (xix. 34) where one of the soldiers with a spear pierced the side of Jesus. Why? (36) "That the Scripture might be fulfilled.... 'They shall look on him whom they pierced.'" Here is the "highly evolved prophetic gnosis" without any disguise. If one writer prefer to fulfil one part of Scripture, the other may select another without much difference in standing. Even Mr. Harris admits that "the gnosis on which Barnabas works is ultimately based on the same passage" as that quoted as fulfilled in the fourth Gospel137; then what distinction of date is possible when both apply the same gnosis based on the same texts?

XI

We have now discussed practically all the test instances advanced by Mr. Rendel Harris, and the result at which we arrive is, that he has not succeeded in proving that the Gospel of Peter betrays such traces of a "highly evolved prophetic gnosis" as require us to assign to it a later date than the canonical Gospels. If this system of elaborate and perverted ingenuity were applied to these Gospels, as it has been to the fragment, and every kind of false exegesis, childish reasoning, and wild interpretation, such as was current amongst the Fathers, brought forward to explain the construction of the four canonical works, the consequence would be terribly surprising to pious readers. That this exegesis began early is quite undeniable, and it is not too much to say that it is palpably visible on the very surface of most of the books of the New Testament. It had, as Mr. Harris must admit and does admit, practical effect on the composition of the Gospels as they have come down to us, but it is fully displayed in some of the Epistles of Paul, still more in those passing under his name, is supreme in the Epistle to the Hebrews, and as for the Acts, the Apostles are, from the very opening, made to express the highly evolved prophetic gnosis of the author. We do not, of course, argue that the writer of the fragment is free from it, but merely that he shares it equally with the other Evangelists, however much their canonicity, derived from the very Fathers who are steeped in this gnosis, may protect them from Mr. Harris's dangerous attack. Without going into an explanation of the genesis of various important points in the story, which would require a volume, we may just glance at some of the points at which the Evangelists frankly declare the source of the gnosis, and allow the process to be seen.

Let us take for instance the first Synoptic. The events previous to the birth of Jesus (i. 18 if.) take place "that it might be fulfilled which was spoken by the Lord through the prophet, saying, Behold, the virgin shall be with child, and shall bring forth a son, And they shall call his name Immanuel," and it is only an illustration of the naïveté of the period that two verses further on they call the son, not Immanuel, but Jesus. The chief priests and scribes inform Herod (ii. 5 f.) that the Christ should be born in Bethlehem of Judaea, because it was written by the prophet: "And thou Bethlehem, land of Judah, Art in no wise least among the princes of Judah: For out of thee shall come forth a governor, Which shall be shepherd of my people Israel." Joseph takes the young child and his mother into Egypt (ii. 15 f.), "that it might be fulfilled which was spoken by the Lord through the prophet, saying, Out of Egypt did I call my son." Herod slays all the male children in Bethlehem and in all the borders thereof (ii. 16 f.) and "then was fulfilled that which was spoken through Jeremiah the prophet, saying, A voice was heard in Ramah, Weeping and great mourning, Rachel weeping for her children," &c. On returning from Egypt they settle in Galilee, in a city called Nazareth (ii. 23), "that it might be fulfilled which was spoken by the prophets, that he should be called a Nazarene." John the Baptist comes preaching "in the wilderness" (iii. 1 f.), "for this is he that was spoken of by Isaiah the prophet, saying, The voice of one crying in the wilderness," &c. The temptation of Jesus in the wilderness is based upon three texts: (iv. 1 ff.) "Man shall not live by bread alone," &c.; "He shall give his angels charge concerning thee," &c., and "Thou shalt worship the Lord thy God," &c. When John is delivered up (iv. 12 ff.) Jesus leaves Nazareth and dwells "in Capernaum, which is by the sea, in the borders of Zebulun and Naphtali: that it might be fulfilled which was spoken by Isaiah the prophet, saying, The land of Zebulun and the land of Naphtali, toward the sea, beyond Jordan, Galilee of the Gentiles, the people which sat in darkness saw a great light, and to them which sat in the region and shadow of death, to them did light spring up." In the episode of John in prison sending his disciples to Jesus (xi. 2 ff.), the whole reply is based indirectly on prophetic gnosis, and the v. 10 directly: "This is he, of whom it is written, Behold, I send my messenger before thy face, Who shall prepare thy way before thee," and v. 14, "And if ye are willing to receive it, this is Elijah, which is to come." When the Pharisees take counsel to destroy him (xii. 14 f.), and Jesus withdraws, healing the sick and enjoining them that they should not make him known, it is "that it might be fulfilled which was spoken by Isaiah the prophet, saying, Behold my servant," &c. There is an exhibition of "highly evolved prophetic gnosis" (xii. 39 ff.) when a sign is asked for, and the sign of Jonah the prophet is given, "for as Jonah was three days and three nights in the belly of the whale, so shall the Son of man be three days and three nights in the heart of the earth," a gnosis which helped to shape the representation of the entombment. The speaking in parables is justified, not originated (xiii. 14 f.), as a fulfilment of the prophecy of Isaiah, "By hearing ye shall hear, and shall in no wise understand," &c, and (v. 35) "I will open my mouth in parables," &c. Of course, as Mr. Harris says, "no sane person would take St. Matthew's quotation as the cause of the Sermon on the Mount, or the parabolic discourse;"138 but, as he admits, the prophetic passages were in the author's mind, and are amongst "the first faint shadows cast by the prophecy [?] upon the history," and they certainly led to the representation that those who heard the parabolic teaching, and notably the disciples, did not understand the most luminous discourses, and required a private explanation of the clearest allegories. The entry into Jerusalem (xxi. 2 f.) is arranged "that it might be fulfilled which was spoken by the prophet, saying, Tell ye the daughter of Zion, Behold, thy King cometh unto thee, meek, and riding upon an ass, and upon a colt the foal of an ass;" and the writer, not appreciating the duplication of Hebrew poetry, is literal enough to relate (v. 2) that Jesus tells the disciples they shall find "an ass tied, and a colt with her," which they are to bring, and (v. 7) "they brought the ass and the colt, and put on them their garments; and he sat upon them" (ἐπάνω αὐτῶν): a representation which has ever since given much trouble to pious commentators. It is not difficult to see that the "cleansing of the temple" (xxi. 12 f.) takes place because "it is written, My house shall be called a house of prayer, but ye make it a den of robbers." The trials when "the abomination of desolation (xxiv. 16 f.), which was spoken of by Daniel the prophet," is seen "standing in the holy place (let him that readeth understand)," is an example of the prophetic gnosis. The preparation for the passion commences (xxvi. 2), "Ye know that after two days the passover cometh, and the Son of man is delivered up to be crucified." Jesus is represented (v. 31) as saying to the disciples: "All ye shall be offended in me this night: for it is written, I will smite the shepherd, and the sheep of the flock shall be scattered abroad;" and the curious phrase which follows is worth consideration: "But after I am raised up, I will go before you into Galilee," which seems to have slipped in here out of its place. The events which take place at the arrest, and their coming out with swords and staves as against a robber to take him (xxvi. 66), "All this is come to pass that the Scriptures of the prophets might be fulfilled;" and Jesus could not pray for legions of angels to help him, for (v. 66), "How then could the Scriptures be fulfilled?" The conduct of Judas after he had betrayed his master, when he took back the pieces of silver, the price of his betrayal, to the priests (xxvii. 3 f.), fulfils "that which was spoken by Jeremiah the prophet, saying, And they took the thirty pieces of silver, the price of him that was priced, whom certain of the children of Israel did price; and they gave them for the potter's field, as the Lord appointed me."

XII

This need not be further pursued, however, though the principle applies quite as much to the other Gospels. Only one passage may be quoted from the last chapter of the third Synoptic. Jesus, when he appears to the disciples, after the episode of the fish to prove that he is not a spirit, but himself with flesh and bones (xxiv. 36 f.), is represented as saying:

These are my words which I spake unto you, while I was yet with you, how that all things must needs be fulfilled, which are written in the law of Moses, and the prophets, and the psalms, concerning me. Then opened he their mind, that they might understand the Scriptures; and he said unto them, Thus it is written that the Christ should suffer, and rise again from the dead the third day: and that repentance and remission of sins should be preached in his name unto all the nations.
This is a direct justification of the gnosis, and it is no wonder that we find St. Sylvia, some centuries later, recording the concrete principle upon which Gospel history is written: "Nothing took place which had not been previously foretold, and nothing had been foretold which had not obtained its fulfilment."

In so far as the Gospel according to Peter is concerned, the impartial verdict must be: It is neither better nor worse than the more fortunate works which have found a safe resting-place within the Canon of the Church. It is almost impossible now to judge of these works as we judge the fragment. Centuries of reverence, and individual habit of hearing their contents with docility and with bated criticism, have rendered most of us incapable of judging the effect which a good part of their contents would make upon us if, like the fragment of Akhmîm, they had been freshly discovered yesterday. There is no canonical glamour to veil its shortcomings, and it must not be forgotten that, in this short fragment, we have none of those parts of the Gospel, such as the Sermon on the Mount and some of the parables, which contain so much noble teaching and render the literature so precious. Then, as we have before pointed out, the canonical Gospels, in their greater circulation and in the process of reception by the Church, secured a gradual revision which might have smoothed away any roughness from the Gospel of Peter had it been equally fortunate. The three Synoptic Gospels are so closely dependent on each other, or on the same sources, as to be practically one work; and although this renders all the more remarkable certain indications of selection, some of which we have pointed out, it nevertheless limits our acquaintance with early belief. It is the merit of the fragment that it presents considerable variation in the original sources, and shows us the fluidity of the early reports of that which was supposed to take place during the period which it embraces. We have in it a primitive and less crystallised form of the Christian tradition.

Appendix - Ευαγγελιον Κατα Πετρον

(1) ... τῶν δὲ Ἰουδαίων οὐδεὶς ἐνίψατο τὰς χεῖρας, οὐδὲ Ἡρώδης οὐδ' εἷς τῶν κριτῶν αὐτοῦ; καὶ μὴ βουληθέντων νίψασθαι ἀνέστη Πειλᾶτος. (2) καὶ τότε κελεύει Ἡρώδης ὁ βασιλεὺς παραλημφθῆναι τὸν κύριον, εἰπὼν αὐτοῖς ὅτι Ὅσα ἐκέλευσα ὑμῖν ποιῆσαι αὐτῷ, ποιήσατε. (3) Ἱστήκει δὲ ἐκεῖ Ἰωσὴφ ὁ φίλος Πειλάτου καὶ τοῦ κυρίου, καὶ εἰδὼς ὅτι σταυρίσκειν αὐτὸν μέλλουσιν, ἦλθεν πρὸς τὸν Πειλᾶτον καὶ ᾔτησε τὸ σῶμα τοῦ κυρίου πρὸς ταφήν. (4) καὶ ὁ Πειλᾶτος πέμψας πρὸς Ἡρώδην ᾔτησεν αὐτοῦ τὸ σῶμα. (5) καὶ ὁ Ἡρώδης ἔφη Ἀδελφὲ Πειλᾶτε, εἰ καὶ μή τις αὐτὸν ᾐτήκει, ἡμεῖς αὐτὸν ἐθάπτομεν, ἐπεὶ καὶ σάββατον ἐπιφώσκει; γέγραπται γὰρ ἐν τῷ νόμῳ ἥλιον μὴ δῦναι ἐπὶ πεφονευμένῳ.

(6) Καὶ παρέδωκεν αὐτὸν τῷ λαῷ πρὸ μιᾶς τῶν ἀζύμων, τῆς ἑορτῆς αὐτῶν. οἱ δὲ λαβόντες τὸν κύριον ὤθουν αὐτὸν τρέχοντες, καὶ ἔλεγον Σύρωμεν τὸν υἱὸν τοῦ θεοῦ, ἐξουσίαν αὐτοῦ ἐσχηκότες. (7) καὶ πορφύραν αὐτὸν περιέβαλλον, καὶ ἐκάθισαν αὐτὸν ἐπὶ καθέδραν κρίσεως, λέγοντες Δικαίως κρῖνε, βασιλεῦ τοῦ Ἰσραήλ. (8) καὶ τις αὐτῶν ἐνενκὼν στέφανον ἀκάνθινον ἔθηκεν ἐπὶ τῆς κεφαλῆς τοῦ κυρίου. (9) καὶ ἕτεροι ἑστῶτες ἐνέπτυον αὐτοῦ ταῖς ὄψεσι, καὶ ἄλλοι τὰς σιαγόνας αὐτοῦ ἐράπισαν; ἕτεροι καλάμῳ ἔνυσσον αὐτόν, καί τινες αὐτὸν ἐμάστιζον λέγοντες Ταύτῃ τῇ τιμῇ τιμήσωμεν τὸν υἱὸν τοῦ θεοῦ.

(10) Καὶ ἤνενκον δύο κακούργους, καὶ ἐσταύρωσαν ἀνὰ μέσον αὐτῶν τὸν κύριον; αὐτὸς δὲ ἐσιώπα, ὡς μηδὲν πόνον ἔχων. (11) καὶ ὅτε ὤρθωσαν τὸν σταυρόν, ἐπέγραψαν ὅτι Οὗτός ἐστιν ὁ βασιλεὺς τοῦ Ἰσραήλ. (12) καὶ τεθεικότες τὰ ἐνδύματα ἔμπροσθεν αὐτοῦ διεμερίσαντο, καὶ λαχμὸν ἔβαλον ἐπ' αὐτοῖς. (13) εἷς δέ τις τῶν κακούργων ἐκείνων ὠνείδισεν αὐτοὺς λέγων Ἡμεῖς διὰ τὰ κακὰ ἃ ἐποιήσαμεν οὕτω πεπόνθαμεν, οὗτος δὲ σωτὴρ γενόμενος τῶν ἀνθρώπων τί ἠδίκησεν ὑμᾶς; (14) καὶ ἀγανακτήσαντες ἐπ' αὐτῷ ἐκέλευσαν, ἵνα μὴ σκελοκοπηθῇ, ὅπως βασανιζόμενος ἀποθάνοι.

(15) Ἦν δὲ μεσημβρία, καὶ σκότος κατέσχε πᾶσαν τὴν Ἰουδαίαν; καὶ ἐθορυβοῦντο, καὶ ἠγωνίων μή ποτε ὁ ἥλιος ἔδυ, ἐπειδὴ ἔτι ἔζη; γέγραπται γὰρ αὐτοῖς ἥλιον μὴ δῦναι ἐπὶ πεφονευμένῳ. (16) καί τις αὐτῶν εἶπεν Ποτίσατε αὐτὸν χολὴν μετὰ ὄξους; (17) καὶ κεράσαντες ἐπότισαν. καὶ ἐπλήρωσαν πάντα, καὶ ἐτελείωσαν κατὰ τῆς κεφαλῆς

αὐτῶν τὰ ἁμαρτήματα. (18) περιήρχοντο δὲ πολλοὶ μετὰ λύχνων, νομίζοντες ὅτι νύξ ἐστίν; [τινὲς δὲ] ἐπέσαντο.

(19) καὶ ὁ κύριος ἀνεβόησε λέγων Ἡ δύναμίς μου, ἡ δύναμις κατέλειψάς με; καὶ εἰπὼν ἀνελήφθη. (20) καὶ αὐτῆς ὥρας διεράγη τὸ καταπέτασμα τοῦ ναοῦ τῆς Ἰερουσαλὴμ εἰς δύο.

(21) Καὶ τότε ἀπέσπασαν τοὺς ἥλους ἀπὸ τῶν χειρῶν τοῦ κυρίου, καὶ ἔθηκαν αὐτὸν ἐπὶ τῆς γῆς; καὶ ἡ γῆ πᾶσα ἐσείσθη, καὶ φόβος μέγας ἐγένετο. (22) τότε ἥλιος ἔλαμψε καὶ εὑρήθη ὥρα ἐνάτη. (23) ἐχάρησαν δὲ οἱ Ἰουδαῖοι καὶ δεδώκασι τῷ Ἰωσὴφ τὸ σῶμα αὐτοῦ ἵνα αὐτὸ θάψῃ,

(24) ἐπειδὴ θεασάμενος ἦν ὅσα ἀγαθὰ ἐποίησεν. λαβὼν δὲ τὸν κύριον ἔλουσε καὶ εἴλησε σινδόνι καὶ εἰσήγαγεν εἰς ἴδιον τάφον καλούμενον Κῆπον Ἰωσήφ.

(25) Τότε οἱ Ἰουδαῖοι καὶ οἱ πρεσβύτεροι καὶ οἱ ἱερεῖς, γνόντες οἷον κακὸν ἑαυτοῖς ἐποίησαν, ἤρξαντο κόπτεσθαι καὶ λέγειν Οὐαὶ ταῖς ἁμαρτίαις ἡμῶν; ἤγγισεν ἡ κρίσις καὶ τὸ τέλος Ἰερουσαλήμ. (26) ἐγὼ δὲ μετὰ τῶν ἑταίρων μου ἐλυπούμην, καὶ τετρωμένοι κατὰ διάνοιαν ἐκρυβόμεθα; ἐζητούμεθα γὰρ ὑπ' αὐτῶν ὡς κακοῦργοι καὶ ὡς τὸν ναὸν θέλοντες ἐμπρῆσαι. (27) ἐπὶ δὲ τούτοις πᾶσιν ἐνηστεύομεν, καὶ ἐκαθεζόμεθα πενθοῦντες καὶ κλαίοντες νυκτὸς καὶ ἡμέρας ἕως τοῦ σαββάτου.

(28) Συναχθέντες δέ οἱ γραμματεῖς καὶ Φαρισαῖοι καὶ πρεσβύτεροι πρὸς ἀλλήλους, ἀκούσαντες ὅτι ὁ λαὸς ἅπας γογγύζει καὶ κόπτεται τὰ στήθη λέγοντες ὅτι Εἰ τῷ θανάτῳ αὐτοῦ ταῦτα τὰ μέγιστα σημεῖα γέγονεν, ἴδετε ὅτι πόσον δίκαιός ἐστιν; (29) ἐφοβήθησαν οἱ πρεσβύτεροι, καὶ ἦλθον πρὸς Πειλᾶτον δεόμενοι αὐτοῦ καὶ λέγοντες Παράδος ἡμῖν στρατιώτας, (30) ἵνα φυλάξω[μεν] τὸ μνῆμα αὐτοῦ ἐπὶ τρεῖς ἡμέρας, μήποτε ἐλθόντες οἱ μαθηταὶ αὐτοῦ κλέψωσιν αὐτὸν καὶ ὑπολάβῃ ὁ λαὸς ὅτι ἐκ νεκρῶν ἀνέστη, καὶ ποιήσωσιν ἡμῖν κακά. (31) ὁ δὲ Πειλᾶτος παραδέδωκεν αὐτοῖς Πετρώνιον τὸν κεντυρίωνα μετὰ στρατιωτῶν φυλάσσειν τὸν τάφον. καὶ σὺν αὐτοῖς ἦλθον πρεσβύτεροι καὶ γραμματεῖς ἐπὶ τὸ μνῆμα. (32) καὶ κυλίσαντες λίθον μέγαν κατὰ τοῦ κεντυρίωνος καὶ τῶν στρατιωτῶν ὁμοῦ πάντες οἱ ὄντες ἐκεῖ ἔθηκαν ἐπὶ τῇ θύρᾳ τοῦ μνήματος.

(33) καὶ ἐπέχρισαν ἑπτὰ σφραγῖδας, καὶ σκηνὴν ἐκεῖ πήξαντες ἐφύλαξαν. (34) πρωίας δέ, ἐπιφώσκοντος τοῦ σαββάτου, ἦλθεν ὄχλος ἀπὸ Ἱερουσαλὴμ καὶ τῆς περιχώρου ἵνα ἴδωσι τὸ μνημεῖον ἐσφραγισμένον.

(35) Τῇ δὲ νυκτὶ ᾗ ἐπέφωσκεν ἡ κυριακή, φυλασσόντων τῶν στρατιωτῶν ἀνὰ δύο δύο κατὰ φρουράν, μεγάλη φωνὴ ἐγένετο ἐν τῷ οὐρανῷ. (36) καὶ εἶδον ἀνοιχθέντας τοὺς οὐρανοὺς καὶ δύο ἄνδρας κατελθόντας ἐκεῖθεν, πολὺ φέγγος ἔχοντας καὶ ἐγγίσαντας τῷ τάφῳ. (37) ὁ δὲ λίθος ἐκεῖνος ὁ βεβλημένος ἐπὶ τῇ θύρᾳ ἀφ' ἑαυτοῦ κυλισθεὶς ἐπεχώρησε παρὰ μέρος, καὶ ὁ τάφος ἠνοίγη καὶ ἀμφότεροι οἱ νεανίσκοι εἰσῆλθον. (38) ἰδόντες οὖν οἱ στρατιῶται ἐκεῖνοι ἐξύπνισαν τὸν κεντυρίωνα καὶ τοὺς πρεσβυτέρους, παρῆσαν γὰρ καὶ αὐτοὶ φυλάσσοντες; (39) καὶ ἐξηγουμένων αὐτῶν ἃ εἶδον, πάλιν ὁρῶσιν ἐξελθόντας ἀπὸ τοῦ τάφου τρεῖς ἄνδρας, καὶ τοὺς δύο τὸν ἕνα ὑπορθοῦντας, καὶ σταυρὸν ἀκολουθοῦντα αὐτοῖς; (40) καὶ τῶν μὲν δύο τὴν κεφαλὴν χωροῦσαν μέχρι τοῦ οὐρανοῦ, τοῦ δὲ χειραγωγουμένου ὑπ' αὐτῶν ὑπερβαίνουσαν τοὺς οὐρανούς. (41) καὶ φωνῆς ἤκουον ἐκ τῶν οὐρανῶν λεγούσης Ἐκήρυξας τοῖς κοιμωμένοις? (42) καὶ ὑπακοὴ ἠκούετο ἀπὸ τοῦ σταυροῦ ὅτι Ναί. (43) Συνεσκέπτοντο οὖν ἀλλήλοις ἐκεῖνοι ἀπελθεῖν καὶ ἐνφανίσαι ταῦτα τῷ Πειλάτῳ.

(44) καὶ ἔτι διανοουμένων αὐτῶν φαίνονται πάλιν ἀνοιχθέντες οἱ οὐρανοὶ καὶ ἄνθρωπός τις κατελθὼν καὶ εἰσελθὼν εἰς τὸ μνῆμα.

(45) Ταῦτα ἰδόντες οἱ περὶ τὸν κεντυρίωνα νυκτὸς ἔσπευσαν πρὸς Πειλᾶτον, ἀφέντες τὸν τάφον ὃν ἐφύλασσον, καὶ ἐξηγήσαντο πάντα ἅπερ εἶδον, ἀγωνιῶντες μεγάλως καὶ λέγοντες Ἀληθῶς υἱὸς ἦν θεοῦ. (46) ἀποκριθεὶς ὁ Πειλᾶτος ἔφη Ἐγὼ καθαρεύω τοῦ αἵματος τοῦ υἱοῦ τοῦ θεοῦ, ὑμῖν δε τοῦτο ἔδοξεν. (47) εἶτα προσελθόντες πάντες ἐδέοντο αὐτοῦ καὶ παρεκάλουν κελεῦσαι τῷ κεντυρίωνι καὶ τοῖς στρατιώταις μηδὲν εἰπεῖν ἃ εἶδον; (48) συμφέρει γάρ, φασίν, ἡμῖν ὀφλῆσαι μεγίστην ἁμαρτίαν ἔμπροσθεν τοῦ θεοῦ, καὶ μὴ ἐμπεσεῖν εἰς χεῖρας τοῦ λαοῦ τῶν Ἰουδαίων καὶ λιθασθῆναι. (49) ἐκέλευσεν οὖν ὁ Πειλᾶτος τῷ κεντυρίωνι καὶ τοῖς στρατιώταις μηδὲν εἰπεῖν.

(50) Ὄρθρου δὲ τῆς κυριακῆς Μαριὰμ ἡ Μαγδαληνή, μαθήτρια τοῦ κυρίου (φοβουμένη διὰ τοὺς Ἰουδαίους, ἐπειδὴ ἐφλέγοντο ὑπὸ τῆς ὀργῆς, οὐκ ἐποίησεν ἐπὶ τῷ μνήματι τοῦ κυρίου ἃ εἰώθεσαν ποιεῖν αἱ γυναῖκες ἐπὶ τοῖς ἀποθνῄσκουσι καὶ τοῖς ἀγαπωμένοις αὐταῖς;) (51)

λαβοῦσα μεθ' ἑαυτῆς τὰς φίλας ἦλθε ἐπὶ τὸ μνημεῖον ὅπου ἦν τεθείς. (52) καὶ ἐφοβοῦντο μὴ ἴδωσιν αὐτὰς οἱ Ἰουδαῖοι, καὶ ἔλεγον Εἰ καὶ μὴ ἐν ἐκείνῃ τῇ ἡμέρᾳ ᾗ ἐσταυρώθη ἐδυνήθημεν κλαῦσαι καὶ κόψασθαι, καὶ νῦν ἐπὶ τοῦ μνήματος αὐτοῦ ποιήσωμεν ταῦτα. (53) τίς δὲ ἀποκυλίσει ἡμῖν καὶ τὸν λίθον τὸν τεθέντα ἐπὶ τῆς θύρας τοῦ μνημείου, ἵνα εἰσελθοῦσαι παρακαθεσθῶμεν αὐτῷ καὶ ποιήσωμεν τὰ ὀφειλόμενα; (54) μέγας γὰρ ἦν ὁ λίθος, καὶ φοβοῦμεθα μή τις ἡμᾶς ἴδῃ. καὶ εἰ μὴ δυνάμεθα, κἂν ἐπὶ τῆς θύρας βάλωμεν ἃ φέρομεν εἰς μνημοσύνην αὐτοῦ, κλαύσομεν καὶ κοψόμεθα ἕως ἔλθωμεν εἰς τὸν οἶκον ἡμων.

(55) Καὶ ἀπελθοῦσαι εὗρον τὸν τάφον ἠνεῳγμένον; καὶ προσελθοῦσαι παρέκυψαν ἐκεῖ, καὶ ὁρῶσιν ἐκεῖ τινα νεανίσκον καθεζόμενον μέσῳ τοῦ τάφου, ὡραῖον καὶ περιβεβλημένον στολὴν λαμπροτάτην, ὅστις ἔφη αὐταῖς Τί ἤλθατε; τίνα ζητεῖτε; (56) μὴ τὸν σταυρωθέντα ἐκεῖνον; ἀνέστη καὶ ἀπηλθεν; εἰ δὲ μὴ πιστεύετε, παρακύψατε καὶ ἴδατε τὸν τόπον ἔνθα ἔκειτο, ὅτι οὐκ ἔστιν; ἀνέστη γὰρ καὶ ἀπῆλθεν ἐκεῖ ὅθεν ἀπεστάλη. (57) τότε αἱ γυναῖκες φοβηθεῖσαι ἔφυγον.

(58) Ἦν δὲ τελευταία ἡμέρα τῶν ἀζύμων, καὶ πολλοί τινες ἐξήρχοντο, ὑποστρέφοντες εἰς τοὺς οἴκους αὐτῶν, τῆς ἑορτῆς παυσαμένης. (59) ἡμεῖς δὲ οἱ δώδεκα μαθηταὶ τοῦ κυρίου ἐκλαίομεν καὶ ἐλυπούμεθα, καὶ ἕκαστος λυπούμενος διὰ τὸ συμβὰν ἀπηλλάγη εἰς τὸν οἶκον αὐτοῦ. (60) ἐγὼ δὲ Σίμων Πέτρος καὶ Ἀνδρέας ὁ ἀδελφός μου λαβόντες ἡμῶν τὰ λίνα ἀπήλθαμεν εἰς τὴν θάλασσαν; καὶ ἦν σὺν ἡμῖν Λευεὶς ὁ τοῦ Ἀλφαίου, ὃν Κύριος ...

Notes

1. Fragments grecs du Livre d'Enoch, &c., publiés par les membres de la Mission archéol. française à Caire, Fasc. 3, 1893.
2. 1 Fasc.
3. 3 Fasc.
4. The Greek Text will be found in the Appendix.
5. The text of this sentence is faulty.
6. ἡμεῖς γάρ, ἀδελφοί, καὶ Πέτρον καὶ τοὺς ἄλλους ἀποστόλους ἀποδεχόμεθα ὡς Χριστόν; τὰ δὲ ὀνόματι αὐτῶν ψευδεπίγραφα ὡς ἔμπειροι παραιτούμεθα, γινώσκοντες ὅτι τὰ τοιαῦτα οὐ παρελάβομεν. ἐγὼ γὰρ γενόμενος παρ' ὑμῖν ὑπενόουν τοὺς πάντας ὀρθῇ πίστει προσφέρεσθαι; καὶ μὴ διελθὼν τὸ ὑπ' αὐτῶν προφερόμενον ὀνόματι Πέτρου εὐαγγέλιον, εἶπον ὅτι Εἰ τοῦτό ἐστι μόνον τὸ δοκοῦν ὑμῖν παρέχειν μικροψυχίαν, ἀναγινωσκέσθω. νῦν δὲ μαθὼν ὅτι αἱρέσει τινὶ ὁ νοῦς αὐτῶν ἐνεφώλευεν ἐκ τῶν λεχθέντων μοι, σπουδάσω πάλιν γενέσθαι πρὸς ὑμᾶς; ὥστε, ἀδελφοί, προσδοκᾶτέ με ἐν τάχει. ἡμεῖς δέ, ἀδελφοί, καταλαβόμενοι ὁποίας ἦν αἱρέσεως ὁ Μαρκιανός, ὡς καὶ ἑαυτῷ ἠναντιοῦτο μὴ νοῶν ἃ ἐλάλει, ἃ μαθήσεσθε ἐξ ὧν ὑμῖν ἐγράφη. ἐδυνήθημεν γὰρ παρ' ἄλλων τῶν ἀσκησάντων αὐτὸ τοῦτο τὸ εὐαγγέλιον, τουτέστι παρὰ τῶν διαδόχων τῶν καταρξαμένων αὐτοῦ, οὓς Δοκητὰς καλοῦμεν (τὰ γὰρ φρονήματα τὰ πλείονα ἐκείνων ἐστὶ τῆς διδασκαλίας), χρησάμενοι παρ' αὐτῶν διελθεῖν καὶ εὑρεῖν τὰ μὲν πλείονα τοῦ ὀρθοῦ λόγου τοῦ σωτῆρος, τινὰ δὲ προσδιεσταλμένα, ἃ καὶ ὑπετάξαμεν ὑμῖν.—Euseb. H. E. vi. 12.
7. Lods, De Evang. secundum Petrum, 1892, pp. 8 ff.; Harnack, Bruchstücke d. Evang. u.s.w. des Petrus, zweite Aufl. 1893, p. 41; Zahn, Das Ev. des Petrus, 1893, pp. 5 f., 70 ff.; Kunze, Das neu aufgef. Bruchstück des sogen. Petrusev. 1893, pp. 10 f.; Swete, The Akhmîm Fragment of the Apocr. Gospel of St. Peter, 1893, pp. xii f., xliv f.; Hilgenfeld, Zeitschr. wiss. Theol. 1893, ii. Heft. pp. 221 f., 239 ff.; J. Armitage Robinson, B.D., The Gospel according to Peter, &c., 1892, pp. 15 ff.; Martineau, The Nineteenth Century, 1893, pp. 906 ff.; J. R. Harris, Contemp. Rev. August 1893, p. 236; van Manen, Theol. Tijdschr. Juli 1893, p. 385.
8. L.c. p. 4 f.
9. H. E. iii. 16.
10. H. E. iii. 3.
11. Sozom. H. E. vii. 19; Canon Murat. Tregelles, p. 65.
12. H. E. iii. 27.
13. H. E. iii. 3.

14. Comm. in Matt. T. x. 17: τοὺς δὲ ἀδελφοὺς Ἰησοῦ φασί τινες εἶναι, ἐκ παραδόσεωσ ὁρμώμενοι τοῦ ἐπιγεγραμμένου κατὰ Πέτρον εὐαγγελίου,)ἢ τῆσ βίβλου Ἰακώβου, υἱοὺς Ἰωσὴφ ἐκ προτέρας γυναικὸς συνῳκηκυίας αὐτῷ πρὸ τῆς Μαρίας.
15. Cf. Murray, Expositor, January, 1893, pp. 55 ff.
16. De Vir. illustr. i.
17. οἳ δὲ Ναζωραῖοι Ἰουδαῖοί εἰσιν τὸν Χριστὸν τιμῶντες ὡς ἄνθρωπον δίκαιον καὶ τῷ καλουμένῳ κατὰ Πέτρον εὐαγγελίῳ κεχρημένοι. Haer. Fab. ii. 2.
18. Zahn, Gesch. des N. T. Kanons, ii. 742 f.; Lods, l.c. pp. 14 ff. Zahn, however, admits that Theodoret's statement may at least be taken as testimony that the Gospel was in use amongst a sectarian community in Syria. Das Ev. d. Petrus, pp. 70 f.
19. Harnack, l.c. pp. 40 ff.; Zahn, l.c. pp. 57 ff.; J. O. F. Murray, The Expositor, January 1893, pp. 55 ff.; Kunze, l.c. pp. 35 ff.; Hilgenfeld, l.c. pp. 242 ff.; Bernard, Academy, December 1892, September 30, 1893; Swete, l.c. p. xxxi.
20. Academy, October 21, December 23, 1893.
21. Guardian, November 29, 1893.
22. Academy, December 23, 1893, p. 568.
23. The detailed statement of the case may be found in Supernatural Religion, complete ed. 1879, i. 283 ff. Hort (Journal of Philology, iii. 155 ff.) places it as early as a.d. 148.
24. Καὶ τὸ εἰπεῖν μετωνομακέναι αὐτὸν Πέτρον ἕνα τῶν ἀποστόλων, καὶ γεγράφθαι ἐν τοῖς ἀπομνημονεύμασιν αὐτοῦ γεγενημένον καὶ τοῦτο, μετὰ τοῦ καὶ ἄλλους δύο ἀδελφούς, υἱοὺς Ζεβεδαίου ὄντας, μετωνομακέναι ὀνόματι τοῦ Βοανεργές, ὅ ἐστιν υἱοὶ βροντῆς, κ.τ.λ. Dial. cvi. The whole argument may be found in detail in Supernatural Religion, 1879, i. 416 ff.
25. See the argument, Supernatural Religion, i. 448 ff.
26. Οἱ γὰρ ἀπόστολοι ἐν τοῖς γενομένοις ὑπ' αὐτῶν ἀπομνημονεύμασιν, ἃ καλεῖται εὐαγγέλια, κ.τ.λ. Apol. i. 66.
27. Eusebius, H. E. iii. 39.
28. Dial. xxiii., xliii. twice, xlv. thrice, c. twice, ci., cxx.; Apol. i. 32 cf. Supernatural Religion, i. 300 f.
29. Luke ii. 4.
30. Dial. lxxviii.
31. Protevang. Jacobi, x.; Tischendorf, Evang. Apocr. p. 19 f.
32. Cf. Supernatural Religion, i. 304 f.
33. Apol. i. 40.

34. The word used in the Gospel is σύρω, to drag along, but Justin's word is merely the same verb with the addition of δια, διασύρω, to worry, or harass with abuse. Although the English equivalent is thus changed, and conceals the analogy of the two passages, the addition of δια, strictly considered, cannot so change the meaning of σύρω, but rather should imply a continuance of the same action. This is also Dr. Martineau's view.
35. Καὶ γάρ, ὡς εἶπεν ὁ προφήτης, διασύροντες αὐτὸν ἐκάθισαν ἐπὶ βήματος καὶ εἶπον; Κρῖνον ἡμῖν. Apol. i. 35.
36. Ἔλεγον, Σύρωμεν τὸν υἱὸν τοῦ θεοῦ, ... καὶ ἐκάθισαν αὐτὸν ἐπὶ καθέδραν κρίσεως, λέγοντες Δικαίως κρῖνε, βασιλεῦ τοῦ Ἰσραήλ. Evang. Petri, 6. Hilgenfeld says regarding this, "Was fehlt noch zu dem Beweise, dass Justinus, wie ich schon 1850 ausgeführt habe, das Petrus-Evg. benutzt hat?" Zeitschr. 1893, ii. 251.
37. This passage has been discussed at some length by Dr. Martineau (Nineteenth Century, October 1893, pp. 647 ff.), in controversy with Mr. T. Rendel Harris (Contemp. Rev. August 1893, pp. 234 ff.), as it has frequently before been. Dr. Martineau seems to be in the right upon all points in connection with it.
38. Hilgenfeld, Zeitschr. wiss. Theol. 1893, pp. 249 ff.; cf. Lods, De Evang. sec. Petrum, pp. 12 f.; Harnack, l.c. pp. 38 f., 63 f.; Martineau, Nineteenth Century, October 1893, pp. 650 f.; cf. Swete, l.c. p. xxxiv.
39. Dial. xcvii.
40. Swete, l.c. p. xxxiv. Mr. Rendel Harris says: "I regard it as certain that the reading λαχμὸς implies connection between Justin and Peter, either directly or through a third source accessible to both." Contemp. Rev. August 1893, p. 231.
41. Apol. i. 50.
42. Μετὰ γὰρ τὸ σταυρωθῆναι αὐτὸν οἱ σὺν αὐτῷ ὄντες μαθηταὶ αὐτοῦ διεσκεδάσθησαν, μέχρις ὅτου ἀνέστη ἐκ νεκρῶν. Dial. liii.; cf. Supernatural Religion, i. 330 ff.
43. Dial. ciii.
44. Dial. cviii.
45. Cf. Supernatural Religion, i. 339.
46. Cf. Irenaeus, Adv. Haer. iii. 12.
47. Dial. lxxxviii.; cf. Supernatural Religion, i. 316 ff.
48. Dial. ciii. There is another passage in Dial. cxxv., which may be compared: Ἀλλ' ἐπεὶ καὶ ναρκᾶν ἔμελλε, τουτέστιν ἐν πόνῳ καὶ ἐν ἀντιλήψει τοῦ πάθους, ὅτε σταυροῦσθαι ἔμελλεν, ὁ Χριστὸς ὁ ἡμέτερος, κ.τ.λ.
49. Mr. Murray, for instance, quotes a passage from Origen, using a similar expression to that in our fragment, that Jesus was silent as suffering

no pain, with a comment which shows that he did not suspect a Docetic interpretation. Expositor, January 1893, pp. 55 f.
50. Harnack, l.c. pp. 38 ff.; Lods, l.c. pp. 12 f.; Hilgenfeld, Zeitschr. wiss. Theol. 1893, pp. 221, 241, 267; van Manen, Theol. Tijdschrift, 1893, pp. 385 f., 551 ff.; Martineau, Nineteenth Century, June 1893, p. 910, October, pp. 643 f.; cf. J. Rendel Harris, Contemp. Rev. August 1893, pp. 227 ff., 231.
51. Cf. Swete, l.c. pp. xxxiii. ff.
52. Verse 16.
53. Verse 27.
54. Verse 28.
55. Mr. Murray points out that Origen likewise regards the "gall" as baleful, as he likewise represents with our fragment the breaking of the limbs as an act of mercy (Expositor, January 1892, pp. 56 f.). Hilgenfeld is quite convinced that the Epistle derives the passage from Peter (Zeitschr. 1893, ii. 255 f.).
56. The whole passage may be given here, as arguments are founded upon it: Ἀλλὰ καὶ σταυρωθεὶς ἐποτίζετο ὄξει καὶ χολῇ; ἀκούσατε πῶς περὶ τούτου πεφανέρωκαν οἱ ἱερεῖς τοῦ ναοῦ. γεγραμμένης ἐντολῆς; Ὃς ἂν μὴ νηστεύσῃ τὴν νηστείαν, θανάτῳ ἐξολεθρευθήσεται, ἐνετείλατο κύριος, ἐπεὶ καὶ αὐτὸς ὑπὲρ τῶν ἡμετέρων ἁμαρτιῶν ἔμελλεν τὸ σκεῦος τοῦ πνεύματος προσφέρειν θυσίαν, ἵνα καὶ ὁ τύπος ὁ γενόμενος ἐπὶ Ἰσαὰκ τοῦ προσενεχθέντος ἐπὶ τὸ θυσιαστήριον τελεσθῇ. τί οὖν λέγει ἐν τῷ προφήτῃ? Καὶ φαγέτωσαν ἐκ τοῦ τράγου τοῦ προσφερομένου τῇ νηστείᾳ ὑπὲρ πασῶν τῶν ἁμαρτιῶν. προσέχετε ἀκριβῶς καὶ φαγέτωσαν οἱ ἱερεῖς μόνοι πάντες τὸ ἔντερον ἄπλυτον μετὰ ὄξους. πρὸς τί? ἐπειδὴ ἐμέ, ὑπὲρ ἁμαρτιῶν μέλλοντα τοῦ λαοῦ μοῦ τοῦ καινοῦ προσφέρειν τὴν σάρκα μου, μέλλετε ποτίζειν χολὴν μετὰ ὄξους, φάγετε ὑμεῖς μόνοι, τοῦ λαοῦ νηστεύοντος καὶ κοπτομένου ἐπὶ σάκκου καὶ σποδοῦ, κ.τ.λ. (vii. 3-5).
57. Harnack finds it almost certain that the Didache made use of this Gospel (l.c. pp. 58 f., 80); so also van Manen (Theol. Tijdschr. September 1893, pp. 353 f.) and others.
58. L.c. pp. xxi f.
59. L.c. pp. xxii f.
60. L.c. p. xxii, n. 1.
61. L.c. p. xxiv.
62. A Popular Account of the newly recovered Gospel of Peter, 1893, pp. v, f.
63. Ib. p. 75.

64. Ib. p. 76. It should be stated that the Syriac version of Cureton to Luke xxiii. 48 gives nearly this sentence, and that the old Latin Codex of St. Germain reads: "dicentes: Vae nobis, quae facta sunt hodie propter peccata nostra; appropinquavit enim desolatio Hierusalem." Mr. Harris of course refers to these passages. Harnack considers that this passage is derived from our Gospel according to Peter (l.c. p. 57).

65. L.c. p. 81. It may be well to give the passage now in Moesinger's work: " 'Vae fuit, vae fuit nobis, Filius Dei erat hic.' Quum autem eis sol naturalis defecisset, tunc per istas tenebras eis lucidum fiebat, excidium urbis suae advenisse: 'venerunt, ait, judicia dirutionis Jerosolymorum.' Quia itaque haec urbs non recepit eum qui eam aedificaverat, restabat ei ut ruinam suam videret." Evang. Concord. Expositio, 1876, pp. 245 f.

66. L.c. p. 78.

67. L.c. pp. 81 f.

68. L.c. pp. 83 f. Cf. Zahn, l.c. p. 65. Zahn considers it in the highest degree improbable that this was taken by Tatian from Peter, but the improbability is by no means made out.

69. L.c. pp. 82 f.

70. Contemp. Rev. August 1893, p. 236.

71. Ev. Concor. Expos. p. 245.

72. Lods (before a.d. 150), Ev. sec. Petrum, 1893, pp. 26 f.; Robinson (before a.d. 160), The Gospel according to Peter, &c., 1892, p. 32; Harnack (beginning of second century), l.c. p. 80; Zahn (a.d. 140-145), Das Ev. des Petrus, 1893, p. 75; Kunze (about a.d. 170), Das neu aufgefund. Bruchstück des sogen. Petrusev. 1893, p. 47; Hilgenfeld (end of first century), Zeitschr. 1893, pp. 266 f.; Swete (a.d. 150-165), The Akhmîm Fragment, 1893, p. xlv; von Schubert (soon after middle of second century), Die Comp. des Pseudopetr. Ev. Fragments, 1893, p. 195; W. C. van Manen (older, rather than later, than our Gospels), Theol. Tijdschr. 5de Stuk, 1893, pp. 565 ff.; Martineau (a.d. 130), Nineteenth Century, June 1893, p. 925, September, p. 633; J. Rendel Harris (no objection to a.d. 130), Contemp. Rev. August 1893, p. 236.

73. Zahn, l.c. pp. 18 ff.; Swete, l.c. pp. xliii, f.

74. Zahn considers ὁ κύριος inauthentic in this place, but it stands in A C D, and many other codices, and it is adopted by the Revisers of the N. T.

75. Although this is not part of the Gospel, it is very ancient.

76. L.c. p. xliii.

77. L.c. pp. xliii, f.

78. Magn. ix.

79. Cf. Ἀναστὰς δὲ ἀπὸ τοῦ βήματος ἐζήτει ἐξελθεῖν. Evang. Nicod. Pars 1. A. ix. 3; Tischendorf, Evang. Apocr. 1853, p. 229.
80. For the sake of brevity these Gospels will be called simply Matthew, Mark, Luke, and John.
81. Hilgenfeld conjectures that this abrupt mention of Joseph indicates that he must already have been mentioned in the Gospel of Peter. Zeitschr. 1893, 11. Heft, pp. 244 f.
82. Cf. προσελθὼν τῷ Πιλάτῳ ᾐτήσατο τὸ σῶμα τοῦ Ἰησοῦ. Evang. Nicod. Pars I. A. xi. 3; Tischendorf, Evang. Apocr. 1853, p. 234.
83. L.c. pp. 26 f.
84. Zahn, of course, argues that the commands of Herod can only have been given to the previously named Jews, the judges of Jesus, "and perhaps to their servants" (und etwa deren Diener), and he finds fault with Harnack for here bringing in "soldiers" from the canonical Gospels, without warrant from the text. He declares them to be directly excluded by the leading tendency of the Gospel of Peter (l.c. p. 27). This supposed "leading tendency," of hatred of the Jews, is a good deal exaggerated.
85. Zeitschr. 1893, ii. 248 f.
86. Murray, Expositor, January 1893, pp. 55 f.
87. Van Manen conjectures that the author got this "King of Israel" from the independent use of some Hebrew or Aramaic source. Tijdschr. Juli 1893, p. 408.
88. So, for instance, Swete, J. Rendel Harris, Robinson, and others. Others distinctly identify the αὐτῷ with the malefactor: as, for instance, Kunze, l.c. p. 22; Von Schubert, l.c. pp. 28 f.; cf. Lods, l.c. p. 21.
89. L.c. p. 26.
90. "Wer anderer Meinung ist, sollte sie für sich behalten" (l.c. p. 55).
91. Zeitschr. 1893, ii. 254.
92. Van Manen, Theol. Tijdschrift, 4de Stuk, 1893, pp. 408 f.; Martineau, Nineteenth Century, June 1893, p. 911.
93. In the apocryphal work called Anaphora Pilati, an account of the crucifixion supposed to be sent by Pilate to the Emperor Tiberius, Pilate is represented as describing the darkness which comes over the whole earth, and saying that the Emperor could not be ignorant "that in all the world they lighted lamps from the sixth hour until evening" (ὅτι ἐν παντὶ τῷ κόσμῳ ἦψαν λύχνους ἀπὸ ἕκτης ὥρας ἕως ὀψίας). Anaphora Pilati, B. 7; Tischendorf, Evang. Apocr. 1853, p. 423.
94. With regard to this addition of Luke, we may refer to a very interesting letter of Dr. Abbott's in the Spectator of October 21, 1893, from which we take the liberty of extracting the following passage: "In Luke (xxiii.

45) the correct reading is τοῦ ἡλίου ἐκλειπόντος, of which the natural interpretation is, the sun being eclipsed. Now, as it was well known that an eclipse could only happen at new moon, and as Passover was at full moon, this would involve a portentous miracle. The probability is that Luke, who was by no means afraid of miracles, meant a miracle here. Not content with saying (with the Synoptics) 'darkness came over all the land,' he adds, in order to show that the darkness was miraculous, 'the sun being eclipsed.' But is this eclipse 'an invention of a conscious or unconscious romancer'? An examination of the parallel passages in Mark and Matthew will show that it is not. There we find that Jesus uttered a cry to God as abandoning Him. These words caused difficulty from the first. The words 'my God' were rendered by some (e.g. the Gospel of Peter) 'my Power;' by the fourth Gospel the words were omitted; our oldest manuscripts exhibit many variations: ἠλι, ἠλει, ἐλωι; the very bystanders are said to have interpreted the words as referring to Elias failing to help. Now 'Elias failing to help' might be, in Greek, ἠλείου ἐκλειπόντος, or quite as often ἠλίου ἐκλειπόντος, i.e. the sun being eclipsed. It seems extremely probable, then, that Luke is not here 'inventing' a miracle, but suggesting, or adopting, an edifying and miraculous interpretation of what seemed to him a non-edifying tradition" (pp. 546 f.).

95. Or "Why didst thou forsake me?"
96. Dem. Ev. x. 8, p. 494.
97. It is suggested that these words must be taken as sarcasm on the part of those who give the body to Joseph.
98. Harnack suggests that perhaps in the author's time Joseph's garden was a known locality (l.c. p. 28).
99. The Syriac version of Cureton has nearly the same reading.
100. Zeitschr. 1893, ii. 246.
101. It will be remembered that the same accusation is brought against Stephen in Acts. The mockery of the passers-by (Matt. xxvii. 40), "Thou that destroyest the temple, and buildest it in three days, save thyself," is also in the same vein.
102. There is an interesting discussion of the question by Van Manen, Theol. Tijdschr. 1893, 4de Stuk, pp. 423 ff.
103. L.c. p. 28.
104. Dr. Swete also takes this view of the passage, l.c. p. 15, n. 4.
105. There are, of course, many instances of such exaggeration: Apoc. x. 1 f.; Hermas, Sim. ix. 6; 4 Esdras, ii. 43; Passio Perp. c. 10.
106. L.c. p. 70.

107. Cf. Justin, Apol. i. 55: Dial. lxxxvi. xci.; Irenaeus, C. Haer. ii. 24, 4; v. 17, 3 f. In the Ev. Nicod. ii. (Lat. B), in which the descent is fully treated, Jesus Christ is begged to make the sign of the cross: "Et factum est ita, posuitque dominus crucem suam in medio inferni, quae est signum victoriae et usque in aeternum permanebit" (Evang. Nicodemi, Pars ii. Latine B. cap. x. (xxvi.); Tischendorf, Evang. Apocr. 1853, p. 409; Ep. Barn. c. 12; Greg. Nyss. Adv. Jud. c. 7).
108. Constitt. App. viii. 12, pp. 259, 13 f.
109. The expression is so peculiar that we give it in the original.
110. L.c. pp. 263 f. Dr. Martineau translates the passage: "Hast thou preached obedience to them that sleep?" Nineteenth Century, June 1893, pp. 917 f.
111. Harnack, l.c. pp. 68 f.; Lods, l.c. p. 48, although with a ?; Zahn, l.c. pp. 22 f.; Robinson, l.c. pp. 24 f.; Swete, l.c. pp. xiv. 19. (Dr. Swete considers any reference to 1 Pet. iii. 19 improbable.) J. Rendel Harris, l.c. pp. 51 f., 89; von Schubert, l.c. pp. 101 f.; cf. van Manen, l.c. pp. 522 f.; Martineau, l.c. pp. 917 f.
112. Dem. Ev. 500. This is referred to by Dr. Swete, l.c. p. 19, n. 2.
113. For instance, Ignat. Ep. Magn. 9; Hermas, Sim. ix. 16.
114. Dial. lxxii.
115. Haer. iii. 20, 4; iv. 22, 1; 33, 1, 12; v. 31, 1.
116. L.c. p. 52.
117. Westcott and Hort put these words between double brackets, as almost certain interpolations, through the action of "Western influences."
118. The Gospel according to Peter, p. 29, n. 1.
119. In the passage 1 Cor. xi. 23 mention is made of a betrayal: "in the night in which he was betrayed," but without further detail, and it is quite consistent to suppose that the "betrayal" is not attributed to one of the Twelve. However, there is considerable reason for believing that this passage is an interpolation. It is a fact that a betrayal is not alluded to in any other place where we might expect to find it in these Epistles; e.g. Rom. iv. 25; viii. 32; Gal. ii. 20.
120. Harnack argues at considerable length that the Gospel according to Peter must have contained the episode of the woman taken in adultery, inserted into the fourth Gospel.
121. Contemp. Rev. August 1893, p. 217.
122. L.c. pp. 213 f.
123. L.c. p. 215.
124. L.c. p. 216.
125. L.c. p. 216.

126. Dial. lxiv.
127. L.c. pp. 219 ff.
128. L.c. pp. 221 ff.
129. E.g. Matt. xii. 45; xv. 34, 37; xxii. 25 f.; Mark viii. 5, 8; xii. 20 ff.; xvi. 9; Luke ii. 36; viii. 2; xi. 26; xx. 29 f.
130. L.c. p. 222.
131. Apoc. v. 1 ff.
132. L.c. p. 224.
133. Ibid.
134. This is not expressed in the text, which Mr. Harris rather strains for his purpose. The correct reading is: "We were fasting, and we sat mourning and weeping," καὶ ἐκαθεζόμεθα πενθοῦντες καὶ κλαίοντες.
135. L.c. pp. 224 f.
136. Barnabas, 7.
137. L.c. p. 226.
138. L.c. pp. 315 f.

Made in the USA
Middletown, DE
24 July 2019